Family Matters

A Mark Landry Novel

By
Randall H. Miller

D1371993

Table of Contents

Glossary

Active measures	Soviet/Russian term for collection of intelligence and disinformation campaigns to influence politics
Backtrack	A comprehensive suite of professional cybersecurity tools
BOLO	A direct attempt to defeat an encryption algorithm
Cold boot attack	Freezing memory chips to delay dissipation of temporary memory long enough to extract needed information
DNI	Director of National Intelligence
EP	Executive Protection
FEMA	Federal Emergency Management Agency
Forty-fives	Card game that originated in Ireland, popular in the Merrimack Valley of Massachusetts and southern New Hampshire
FSB	Federal Security Service of the Russian Federation
HNWI	High Net Worth Individual
Honeypot	Decoy computer server setup to collect and gather information on cyber threats
HRT	Hostage Rescue Team
Interpol Black alert	Used to seek information on unidentified bodies
Interpol Blue alert	Used to locate, identify, or obtain information on a person of interest in a criminal investigation
Karambit	Southeast Asian curved knife resembling a claw
Keylogger	Program that records every keystroke on a computer, often used to covertly steal passwords and other sensitive information

LEO	Law Enforcement Officer
MEMA	Massachusetts Emergency Management Agency
MICE	Motives for Spying: Money, Ideology, Coercion, Extortion
Netstat	Computer utility tool used to measure traffic on a network
NSA	National Security Agency
OPSEC	Operational Security
Pen test	Penetration Test
Polezni durak	Useful idiot
Psyops	Psychological Operations
RUENB	Russian Embassy
Schengen Agreement	Treaty which led to open borders within European Union Member States
SCIF	Sensitive Compartmented Information Facility
SSCI	Senate Select Committee on Intelligence
SD	Surveillance Detection
SDR	Surveillance Detection Route
SFOD-D	Special Forces Operational Detachment Delta (aka Delta Force)
SVR	Foreign Intelligence Service of the Russian Federation
TATP	Triacetone triperoxide, Explosive (aka Mother of Satan)
Thief-in-law	Originating in the early Soviet Union's prison camps, a title denoting high status of a professional criminal within Russian organized crime
Veiligheid van de Staat	Belgian State Security Services
VR	Virtual Reality
Zelonyye lyudishki	Little Green Men

...

"With a lie you can go very far, but you can never go back." –Anonymous proverb

...

Prelude

The operator had correctly estimated the distance from the fire escape to the top of the dumpster, but he had not anticipated the smooth layer of ice hiding under a thick, white blanket of fresh powder. The balls of his feet made contact with the slippery surface first; his tailbone and the back of his head followed a split second thereafter.

He bounced and found himself airborne again before landing on the much less forgiving pavement with a muted thud, his right knee absorbing much of the impact. He immediately rolled to his back and pulled his knee into his chest with both hands. With two feet of snow on the ground—and counting—it was unlikely that anyone would have been outside to see him. But sound travels faster and farther on windless, snowy nights. He stifled the impulse to scream out in pain.

He lay still and breathed deeply for several minutes before slowly getting to his feet and dusting off his snow-covered body. He stuffed his hands into the front pockets of his navy blue pea coat to readjust the Smith and Wesson Bodyguard .380 and spare magazines, and to make sure that his secure phone and other items had not tumbled out.

He located his car keys and pulled the thick wool hat down tight around his ears. Then he limped to the end of the alley and turned right onto the main road to find his car.

In spite of the snow, the ride to Providence went much quicker than expected. There were few cars on the road, and most of the trip was down I-95 behind a line of emergency snow plows. He parked several blocks from the strip club in an out-of-the-way lot next to an abandoned warehouse.

When the operator reached the dark intersection, he steadied himself on a street sign with one hand and reached down to assess the damage to his knee with the other. It was as large as a grapefruit and throbbing with intense pain. He rubbed it and looked up to survey the four-way intersection.

Visibility was greatly limited as thick, soft snow continued to pour down silently from the sky. The traffic lights blinked red in all directions. There were no cars or other pedestrians. The roads were unplowed.

He drifted diagonally across the intersection, gingerly high-stepping his way through the snow, trying to protect his bum knee and conserve energy. He knew this was just the commute. The hard part of his impromptu solo mission was still to come.

After four plodding blocks, he stopped at the window of a 24-hour convenience store. The cashier, an old man wearing a snowmobile suit, was sitting behind the counter, resting his chin on top of the cash register. His eyes were closed. Next to him were a laptop and some computer supplies. Bells hanging from a leather strap jingled softly when the operator opened the front door. The old man barely seemed to notice and looked annoyed when the operator placed a pack of gum on the counter.

"Actually, I need the bathroom key first, if you don't mind. I'll take care of the gum afterwards," he said with a muffled voice. Tiny clouds of vapor escaped through his frosted hat as he spoke.

The old man grunted and turned around slowly to retrieve the bathroom key from the far wall. As soon as he turned his back, the operator reached over the counter and grabbed the can of compressed air located between the cash register and laptop. The cashier had barely pulled the bathroom key from its hook when the bells on the door jingled again. The operator was out the door and around the corner by the time he turned around.

He wiped the moisture from the face of his watch with a gloved finger and brought his wrist up to eye level. Brightly glowing orange tritium dots on the watch's hands indicated he had less than five minutes to travel the final block to the strip club and be in position.

He knew he was getting close when the faint sound of club music started to fill the air. Less than a block away, on the opposite side of the street, a single door was propped open and illuminated by a dark purple light. He crossed the street and passed the club slowly, surveying as much of the inside as he could see.

One man was sitting at a small bar on the right. The other four or five stools were empty. The bartender had his back to the man and appeared to be closing out his cash register and counting his tips. In the middle of the room were four or five small, unoccupied tables. Someone was getting a lap dance in the back corner. Against the left wall was the operator's final destination: a thick, plexiglass-encased DJ booth. A tall, thin man wearing a hoodie and matching the target's description was working inside the booth.

He circled the building. The back door was locked. Peering through a window, he saw no movement. He was reasonably sure the only people he might have to deal with were out front. The fiery orange dots on his watch indicated three minutes until show time.

In three minutes the DJ, a Black Hat freelance hacker with no conscience, will establish a secure connection with Russian intelligence to receive his next set of orders. The jobs he gets are not your run-of-the-mill criminal activity. Men willing to do routine stuff are a dime a dozen. This guy is different. He does jobs and facilitates financial transactions for organizations involved in child trafficking, weapons smuggling, narco-trafficking, and snuff movies. He even gave material support to an Islamic terror cell operating in Germany. Zero scruples. His impending orders tonight are expected to include detailed instructions for covert espionage, disinformation, and propaganda teams deployed around the United States.

The operator has one chance to intercept the transfer and steal the decryption key. He has no backup.

The plaintext instructions from the FSB's representative will be encrypted using a sophisticated algorithm. Secure packets of data will fly through multiple foreign servers and middlemen before ultimately landing on the DJ's hard drive. The files themselves are unreadable gibberish. A secret decryption key is needed to translate the gibberish back into readable data.

The DJ has the key. The operator wants the key and has already decided that the world would be a better place without the DJ.

His adrenaline surged as he made his way back around to the front of the club. He countered the physiological response with deep, tactical breaths and stayed focused on breaking down the task at hand—just as his mentor had taught him.

> **Task:** Get decryption key from scumbag
> **Conditions:** Blizzard, poorly lit dive bar, minimal time for area familiarization, armed w/ .380 caliber pistol and a can of compressed air
> **Standards:** Obtain decryption key by force if necessary, and get out of Dodge undetected without further injury to self or anyone else (except said scumbag)

Got it.
The knot on the back of his head stopped throbbing and the pain in his knee subsided as he turned the final corner of the building and passed through the open door.

The bartender was still counting his money. In spite of the throbbing pulse of the blaring music, the man at the bar was sleeping. The dancer in the back was now on her knees, her face buried deep in her seated customer's lap. Inside the DJ box, the tall, dark figure stood motionless, staring directly at the bundled up new arrival.

Showtime.

The operator nodded his head at the DJ. Then he turned his back to face the bartender and mimicked his body language as if they were casually talking. He could feel the DJ's eyes glaring at his back as he gesticulated toward the bartender with his hands as if telling a story. He grabbed a cocktail napkin, tore off two small pieces, and rolled them into makeshift earplugs as he acted out the scene. The bartender shifted his weight back and forth between his aching feet and occasionally nodded his head as he counted. Seeing the apparent interaction made the DJ feel better about the stranger's presence. Noting the time, he refocused his attention on his laptop and initiated the secure connection.

After the downloading of the files was complete, the DJ looked up again and scanned the club. The stranger had left and the man at the bar was still out cold. A few seconds later, the bartender picked up several stacks of cash and walked toward the club's private office in the back of the building. Satisfied that the situation was safe, he began reading the messages.

The operator raised his weapon and aligned his sights on the back of the DJ's hoodie-covered head. Handgun sights are unnecessary, maybe even a distraction for close targets, as in this case. Experienced operators save precious seconds by relying more on intuition and natural reflexes than on mechanical sights. But this was not an experienced operator. He lowered his muzzle to the base of the neck between the shoulder blades momentarily, then quickly returned to the center of the back of the head.

Should I just pop the motherfucker in the back of the head? If I do, will he just drop dead? Will his brains splatter on the laptop? Maybe I'm better off creeping up next to him and popping him in the side of the head. Maybe he'll step back from the machine. But it if he logs out and shuts down the laptop before I get my hands on it, I could be fucked. Need to make a decision. Window of opportunity is closing. Fuck it, just shoot him in the back of the head.

He adjusted his two-handed grip on the compact .380, bent his knees, and took a deep breath. He paused one more time to reassure himself that he would be able to live with the decision to end this man's life. He was the lowest of the low. A facilitator of the worst kind of evil. Utterly irredeemable. A pig of a human being.

And the pig just turned around and pulled a Crocodile Dundee–sized knife from inside his waistband so you probably want to pull the trigger right now!

The report from the pistol was partially muffled by the enclosed structure and electronic dance music being pumped throughout the club. Strobe lights masked the muzzle flash. The cocktail napkin scraps stuffed into his ears had offered some protection, but the shockwaves within the booth still hurt like hell.

The jacked hollow point bullet landed in the soft cartilage of the nose and penetrated several inches into the brain before losing steam.

The DJ dropped his head and his body was starting to lurch forward when the second round penetrated the top of his skull, essentially hitting the on/off switch for good. He collapsed to the floor and lay motionless.

The operator crouched and quickly patted down the dead man's pockets. They were empty.

He stood up and quickly scanned the club. All clear. Things were going smoothly. Then he noticed that the DJ's laptop had somehow closed. The DJ had either slammed it shut prior to making his last stand with the Bowie knife or his hoodie had somehow snagged the laptop's lid. Either way, the machine had been turned off and the operator's chances of retrieving the decryption key and saving the day were decreasing with each passing second.

He pushed the body to the side of the booth and retrieved the can of compressed air from his coat pocket. Then he turned over the laptop and used the dead man's knife to pop open the small plastic door on the bottom and expose the system's RAM chip. Holding the can upside down, he depressed the nozzle and sprayed freezing-cold compressed air over the machine until the memory chip was covered in white frost.

Any data used on a computer is stored in the system's RAM. When the system is powered off, all that information disappears. But depending on the system, that purging of data can take anywhere from seconds to minutes. Cooling down the memory chips to roughly negative 50 degrees Celsius—easily done with an inverted can of compressed air—can slow down the fading of data significantly. During that time, any data on the chip, including encryption keys, can theoretically be accessed and exploited. Hackers call it a cold boot attack.

He used the tip of the knife to dislodge the frozen chip from its position. Then he quickly snapped it into place in his own handheld machine and waited to see if it could read the data.

Come on ... come on ... come on! Read it! Read it!

The screen turned blue, confirming that the chip was readable.

He initiated the process to copy all readable files and slipped the handheld machine back into the deep pocket of his pea coat. Then he stuffed the DJs' laptop and personal belongings into a nearby backpack, verified the status of his weapon, and walked out of the club with the bag slung over his shoulder.

The blizzard was letting up and he crossed paths with one or two plows and salt spreaders on the way to his vehicle. He knew he would have to sit tight and give authorities some time to clear the major roadways before driving back to Boston, but at least he'd be able to start sending information to his colleagues digitally. The laptop itself and the rest of the physical evidence would have to wait until he arrived.

The operator fired up the powerful engine of his 4x4 and scanned the area. Nobody in sight.

He initiated an encrypted connection with the company's secure servers—machines that he had personally installed and configured—and ignored the vibrating phone in his right cargo pocket as long as he could. Finally, he pulled it out and answered without looking at it. He didn't have to look. The same person—Mark Landry—had been calling for the past two hours. He took his phone off Hide mode and answered.

"Go ahead, Mark."

Landry exhaled and paused for a second before speaking. He was clearly pissed.

"Where the hell are you?"

Two weeks earlier

CHAPTER ONE: Roll Call

Mark Landry emerged from the woods in a full sprint. Covered in sweat, his arms and legs pumping, he turned hard left and made his way to the edge of the paved road. He glanced at his watch and smiled.

Not bad.

He slowed his pace for the next half-mile to catch his breath, plan the rest of the day, and prepare for the final uphill sprint that would end the running portion of his workout. Steam rose from his body and quickly dissipated into the cold November air.

When he reached the bottom of the long driveway, he jogged in place for several seconds, shook out his arms, and rolled his head from side to side.

Ready. Set. Go.

Mustering every bit of strength remaining in his legs, Mark sprinted up the long zig-zagging driveway toward the house.

"It would be cheaper to just have the driveway go straight up the hill, Mark. It would also mean fewer trees would have to be cleared. That's all I'm saying," Luci had suggested after they purchased the land and started laying the plans for their home together.

"I get that. But a few turns will make it safer in the snow and ice instead of having to drive straight up and down a hill for a hundred yards. It'll also be a buffer between the house and the rest of the world. When you come home from a long day of work the few extra seconds to get to the house will give you a chance to decompress, right?"

"Okay. Whatever you want, just don't ask me to shovel it," she replied, giving him a soft kiss on the cheek. "But don't think for a second you're fooling me. You're not a landscape architect, Mark. You're a security specialist. You want the Z-shape because it'll slow down any approaching vehicles."

Mark resisted the urge to smile at the memory. He didn't want to waste what little fuel was left in his tank. He would need it for the stairs.

Murphy, the family's three-year old German shepherd, had been waiting patiently in front of the three-stall garage. As soon as Mark crested the hill, Murphy dashed forward and took his place at his master's left side. The two sprinted together to the control panel mounted on the side of the house, and Mark opened the far right garage door.

"You ready, buddy? You ready?"

Murphy crouched low to the ground and barked once.

Mark entered the garage and walked quickly toward the basement entrance. He disarmed the alarm system and flung open the door.

"Go, Murphy! Go!"

The dog took off like a bullet train and was up the stairs before Mark had even crossed the room. At the bottom of the stairs, he dropped to the ground and knocked off fifty pushups as quickly as he could before sprinting to the first floor of the house. Murphy was waiting at the top of the stairs, indicating that he had found no threats on the main floor.

"Good boy, Murphy. Ready, go!"

The dog bolted toward the next staircase and ascended to the second floor. Mark dropped and did fifty crunches as quickly as he could, leaving behind a puddle of sweat on the slate-tiled floor. Murphy was crouched low and waiting for him when he reached the top of the second staircase.

"Wait here," he ordered. Then he made his way down the long hallway and disappeared into a bedroom. He emerged seconds later with a thirty-five-pound sandbag in each arm. "Back door, Murphy! Back door!"

Mark descended the stairs at an operational pace—as swiftly as possible while maintaining complete control. Not too fast, not too slow. Deliberate. Present. Fully aware of the environment and ready to respond to any surprises. At the bottom of the stairs he turned right and headed down the long foyer. Murphy was waiting on the far side of the kitchen, next to the sliding glass door that opened onto the back patio. Mark unlocked the door and slid it open.

"Go! Go!"

Murphy leaped out the door and sprinted around the backyard, scanning for threats, while Mark walked briskly to the center of the yard and dropped the sandbags next to the jungle gym. He reached for the monkey bars and did a quick set of chin-ups on the first rung before negotiating the rest of the bars. When he reached the final bar, he rotated his grip and did one final set of pullups before returning to the first rung and letting go. He shook out his hands and called Murphy to his side.

"Okay, play time. Good job, Murphy! Nice work, buddy. You're a good boy, aren't you?"

The dog basked in his master's praise and rolled onto his back to have his belly rubbed. Mark grabbed a nearby tennis ball and threw it to the far end of the yard. Murphy had the ball in his powerful jaws before the third bounce and was back at Mark's side within seconds.

"Good boy, Murphy! You wanna play a little? Okay, but only for a few minutes. I need to shower and get to work."

Murphy barked and Mark tossed the ball high into the air again.

During his twenty years of service at the highest levels of U.S. special operations, Mark Landry had executed just about every conceivable type of mission, ranging from targeted assassinations, abductions, and hostage rescue to surveillance and counter-surveillance operations. The success of each mission had hinged on three essential characteristics: intense physical conditioning, finely honed skills, and an unwavering commitment to getting the job done.

Mark had been assigned to or volunteered for some of the toughest special operations missions in contemporary history and was well known for his resourcefulness, optimism, and positive attitude. But his closest friends and mission partners all knew there was one type of assignment that he dreaded from start to finish—one situation where he had to simply bite his tongue and force himself to do the work. Mark Landry absolutely hated protective details.

His level of frustration varied according to the specifics of the assignment. Delivering an important person or intelligence asset safely from point A to point B wasn't so bad. Accompanying one of the country's top spooks to a clandestine meeting with his less-than-savory counterpart in a shithole like Somalia or Nigeria was necessary. But Mark bristled at assignments that put him in harm's way for no apparent reason. And he occasionally had a hard time concealing those feelings.

"Can you believe this?" he had once said to Billy, his partner, after they had covertly shadowed a French diplomat through a crowded Istanbul bazaar. "If she's so fucking important, why aren't the French watching over her? And why is she waltzing through a jihadist-infested flea market by herself like she doesn't have a care in the world? Screw this, man. There's gotta be something more important than this going on in the world."

But that was the past. His days of government work were over. In the private security sector, Mark had much more control over his assignments. He looked at his watch and jogged toward the house with a smile on his face. It was time to shower and get ready for the one protection detail he always looked forward to—the only mission he gladly did for free.

Twenty minutes later, the middle garage opened and the supercharged engine of a dark blue Range Rover came to life. The vehicle crept forward and paused at the top of the driveway.

"You ready, Murphy?" he asked over his shoulder.

The dog barked from his perch on the back seat. Mark pressed his foot against the gas pedal and the SUV abruptly lurched forward.

"Then let's get to work."

...

At precisely 1300 hours, Mark opened the door and exited the vehicle. He stuffed his hands into his coat pockets and scanned the area from behind the dark lenses of his miniature aviator sunglasses. A long line of cars was parked along the curb. Multiple pedestrians. Two crosswalk guards with bright orange vests and plastic stop signs in their hands were conversing off to his left. Several folks waved at him. He smiled and nodded his head. He felt exposed.

"The vehicle offers some degree of protection, but never forget that once you break the skin of the vehicle—once you open the door and exit—you and the protectee are most vulnerable," his executive protection instructor had taught him many years ago. Mark glanced back at his Range Rover and recalled explaining the ballistic rating of its windows and side panels to Luci when he drove it home for the first time.

"Seriously, Mark? I don't even want to know how much this cost."

"It didn't cost us anything. It's my second favorite perk of working in the private sector. My favorite is sitting on the back seat. His name is Murphy. You and the kids are going to love him."

The school bell brought Mark's attention back to the present as cars along the curb fired up their engines and the crossing guards started to wrap up their conversation. The dismissal ritual was about to begin. It rarely deviated from the standard pattern.

The director would be the first to appear. He would open one half of the double doors just enough to wave at the crossing guards. This would be their cue to take their positions. Then he would struggle with the doors until a custodian or some other bystander helped him. Once the two doors were open and pinned back against the brick building, he would smile widely at the waiting crowd and, like a circus ringmaster, motion to his staff to start the show.

Several young teaching assistants exited the building first, carrying manila envelopes containing special notes. When they walked past Mark to approach other vehicles, he breathed a sigh of relief. Then a few administrative staff members exited and made beelines to their cars, cell phones pinned against their heads. After a few more seconds, the children began to spill from the schoolhouse. Five-year-old Amanda Landry was usually leading the way.

And there she is …

Amanda exited the door carrying a backpack twice as full as those belonging to the other kids, a determined look on her face. As she walked, she scanned from left to right in search of her dad. When she located him, she stopped in place and smiled widely, looking like a spitting image of her mother, with tan skin, bright white teeth, and soft black hair pulled back into a tight ponytail. She waved and then turned around to face the door and wait patiently for her brother. Carlos Landry eventually emerged from the building just as he had entered the world—several minutes behind his twin sister.

Carlos sat behind the driver's seat and Amanda on the passenger side. Murphy waited for Mark to buckle the kids in before taking his position between the two car seats and licking their faces. They giggled and squirmed as Mark closed Amanda's door and circled around the back of the vehicle. As he fastened his seatbelt and started the engine, a figure appeared in his peripheral vision and approached the vehicle. He unrolled the window.

"Hi, Mr. Landry," said a cheery woman in her mid-forties.

"Hi, Mrs. Greene. Nice to see you."

Mark glanced at Amanda in the rear view mirror. She crossed her arms in front of her chest and scowled in her teacher's direction.

"It's nice to see you too. I know you're probably in a rush, but I was wondering if I'll be seeing you and Sergeant Landry at parent-teacher conferences next week?"

"Luci will be there. Unfortunately, I'll be traveling on business so I can't make it. Is everything okay?" he asked.

"Oh, yes, no worries. I just like to check with all of my parents in advance as a friendly reminder. Just in case they forgot. But there's nothing to worry about. The kids are adjusting pretty well to being in different classrooms, and I think the split has done a lot for Carlos's independence. I'm sure his teacher will have more detailed development feedback for you, but Amanda is doing very well in my room. Aren't you, honey?" she said, waving to her student.

Amanda turned away to look out her window without answering. Mrs. Greene leaned in and lowered the volume of her voice.

"She's telling some pretty tall tales. It's nothing to be alarmed about. All kids this age make things up. But she gets really upset if anyone questions her, and that's a bit concerning."

"What kind of tales?" Mark asked.

"Today was the story about staring down and chasing off two coyotes with a baseball bat again. When the other kids laughed, she took it pretty hard, so I had a talk with her. From now on, she's going to save those kinds of stories for story time on Tuesdays and Thursdays. We encourage the kids to be creative, but it's also important at this age for them to start to distinguish fact from fiction. You understand, right? So you may just want to keep that in mind if she does the same thing at home, okay?"

"Got it, thanks."

"Just one more thing," Mrs. Greene continued. "No pressure. But next month a number of parents have volunteered to come in and read stories to the class or talk about their jobs. We'd love to have you for either. It would be exciting for the kids to hear about what it's like to be a security guard."

It took all of his strength not to wince at the insinuation that he was some type of security guard. "I'll see what I can do."

Mark closed his window and looked up to see Amanda staring at him in the rear-view mirror. He turned his head to the side so as to look his daughter directly in the eyes. Then he smiled and winked at her.

"I'm proud of you, Mandy. Keep up the good work."

As Mark pulled out of the school driveway and headed home, he held up an empty backpack with his right hand.

"What's up with this, Carlos? Why is your backpack empty?"

"I don't know," he answered in a giggle as Murphy licked the side of his neck with his long tongue.

"Could it be because your sister has all your stuff in her pack? This is the last time, Carlos. From now on, you carry all your own gear, got it?"

Carlos folded Murphy's lips onto the top of his snout and exposed his powerful teeth. "I'm going to brush your teeth later, Murphy."

"Did you hear me, little man?" Mark repeated in a slightly raised voice and a more serious tone.

"Yes, Daddy. I heard you."

. . .

Amanda rolled around on the kitchen floor with Murphy and Carlos sat at the table, scribbling with his crayons, while Mark cooked dinner. He added spices and stirred the food. Then he tapped a finger against the monitor above the stove to unmute the news.

"Good evening, and here are tonight's top stories," said the anchor. "First, according to an explosive new bipartisan congressional report, Russia's sphere of influence is now at its greatest since the height of the Cold War. This is in spite of crippling economic sanctions and years of efforts by Western states to contain Russian influence. Predictably, a spokesman for the Kremlin has dismissed the report as baseless anti-Russian propaganda. Here's what Republican Senate Majority Leader Johnson of North Carolina—a close confidant of the President—had to say about the Russian response just moments ago."

The broadcast cut to a clip of the sharply dressed senator descending the stairs of an unmarked private jet at Washington's Dulles International Airport. Johnson had spent the last three decades in office with one eye permanently fixed on intelligence matters. As one of the most influential and respected men in government, he also served as one of the current President's closest advisors on national security and crisis management. He nodded and listened closely to the question, looked directly into the camera, and answered in a strong, confident tone. Johnson was widely known for playing his cards close to his vest. He made few unplanned public statements. When he did, they were substantive.

"Look, the Russians can try to spin this however they want, but the facts remain the facts. And just because they may not have physical troops on the ground throughout what they consider to be their domain, that is completely irrelevant in this day and age. A virtual occupation is still an occupation. Once you're inside another state's digital infrastructure, you have essentially colonized them. How else could you possibly describe one state's control of another's core services, from water and gas to banking and telecommunications? We stand by our assessment: the current size and scope of Russia's sphere of influence represent a major threat to global security. In fact, this is an imminent threat."

Imminent threat? I can help with those, Senator. It's what I do.

"We'll have more on that story from a panel of experts later in the show," said the news anchor. "But before we get to all that, let's start things off with the national weather forecast and threat assessments for the rest of the week."

Mark tapped his finger on the screen to kill the display. He checked his watch and sent a text to Dunbar.

MARK: Will give SITREPs in about an hour. Ghost teams are quiet but our protection detail had action on way back from Philippines. No injuries.
DUNBAR: Copy. Talk then.

"Okay, munchkins. Go wash your paws. It's time to eat."

"Where's Mommy?" asked Carlos.

"The same place she was the last time you asked. She's working. But when she gets home, I'll make sure she goes into your room to kiss you good night, okay?"

"Okay!"

Carlos plunged a fork into his macaroni and cheese and Amanda poured a few drops of dressing onto her salad. Mark sipped his water and smiled.

Great kids.

...

Detective Lieutenant Luci Landry exited I-495 in her unmarked police cruiser and headed north on Route 28 into Lawrence. She adjusted her control panel to monitor local authorities and turned to the young UMass criminal justice student sitting in the passenger seat.

"We'll make a run all the way up Broadway to the New Hampshire border. Then we'll take 213 and swing back around to 495 south. We'll finish the ride-along in Lowell and you'll be back at your dorm long before you turn into a pumpkin. Sound like a plan?"

"Absolutely, whatever you want to do is fine by me," she answered. "I'm just glad to be here with you. It's really nice of you to bring me out into the field. I appreciate it. This task force is all my professor can talk about lately. I think he helped the Governor put it together or something like that."

Luci shook her head and cracked a smile from ear to ear. "Yeah, I know that. You've told me that like ten times already. It's not a big deal. And it's almost over, so if there's anything in particular you want to see or ask me about, now would be the time. So go ahead—ask me anything."

The twenty-year-old sat up straight and smiled. "Okay, how about I put this stuff away and we just talk." She placed the cap on her pen and stowed it in her bag with her spiral-bound notebook. "What's the most frustrating part of the job for you personally, and how do you deal with it? And what are you going to do after retirement in the next few months?"

Luci pursed her lips and nodded her head slowly while she considered the first part of the question and weighed her options. Should she give a safe and simple answer or just tell the truth? The student filled the pause by offering answers of her own.

"Is it prosecutors who drop balls or make ridiculous demands?"

"Ah, no. But that's definitely on the list too."

"Judges, then? Are they all too lenient and soft?"

Luci slowed to a stop at the final traffic light before crossing the Merrimack River and turned toward her guest. "Man, what the hell are they teaching you guys these days? You're not even out of school yet and you're that jaded?"

"Not at all. My professors are all big believers in the system. But I see things in the news and on the Internet too. And these days, you never really know what's true, right? That's one of the reasons I'm here with you in the field. I want to know what it's really like out here."

Once they had crossed the Merrimack River, the number of cars, pedestrians, and sources of loud music gradually increased. "Nah, your professors are right. The system works. You should definitely believe in the system. Sure, some prosecutors and judges make decisions I wouldn't make, but we cops don't always make their jobs easy either. But the biggest challenge is staying positive when ninety percentage of your interactions with people are not for good reasons." She drifted slightly left to get around a line of cars double-parked in front of a dingy guest house.

"I get it."

"I know the job is going to be a grind sometimes. All jobs are a grind to some extent. But that stuff has never bothered me too much because it comes with the territory. No job is perfect. And even though I have seen some thoroughly messed-up things in the system, I still have faith in it. As for society, that's a different story. I can't say I've lost faith in society, but that faith is rattled."

"Why? Specifically, why?"

"Because I see people throw their lives away. And I see people have their lives thrown away by others. Sexual assaults are endless. I've seen some killing. And some days I feel like everyone I talk to is lying to me—because most of them are. So it can be tough to stay positive."

"You make it sound terrible."

"Nah, don't waste too much time thinking on all that. I'm venting a little bit, but those feelings are definitely real. My challenge is keeping them in check by constantly reminding myself that the overwhelming majority of people are not, excuse me, assholes. And I worry I won't be able to do that forever. Which brings us back to the integrity of the system. Is a society full of people like those I've just described worthy of its civil liberties? Or should authorities have more flexibility to crack down when and where they see fit? That would make an interesting essay topic, wouldn't it? Have you chosen the topic for your thesis yet? What do you think?"

After several awkward seconds, Luci turned her head to check on her passenger. She was furiously tapping away on her smartphone with a smile that clearly had nothing to do with the conversation at hand. She hadn't caught any of that last part. Luci shook her head and continued talking out loud, although she knew she was the only one listening.

"As for retirement, I'm not sure yet. I still have a few more months before I have to decide."

And it can't come quickly enough.

...

Senator Lois McDermott of Connecticut stood behind her oak desk and pressed down firmly on the mute button with the eraser side of a standard number 2 pencil. "I need a few minutes alone to wrap things up here. Tell the car to meet me at the back door, ok?"

"You got it," replied the eager aide.

When the door closed, the senator lifted the pencil from the button and dropped it in the top drawer. "Okay. Go ahead. I can talk now. I agree with most of the plan. I'm not crazy about parts of it, but I'm aware security dictates most of the decisions so I won't make a fuss over anything. Okay. Yes, I agree. No problem, then. Speak with you soon. Good evening."

She put on her coat and admired the framed Abigail Adams quotation hanging on the wall behind her desk while wrapping a scarf twice around her neck. "Remember, all men would be tyrants if they could," Abigail had reminded her husband, President John Adams, in one of her famous letters.

Ain't that the truth, Abby.

Two Capitol Police officers escorted her down the hall toward one of the private exits. She paused to check her phone for messages. Meetings, rallies, demonstrations, hearings, press. All work. Nothing else. But what was she expecting? That Mark would just up and invite her over to spend the long holiday weekend with his family out of the blue?

Never say never, Lois. Never say never.

But he had been clear from the moment he appeared unannounced in her living room that publicly acknowledging him as her child was not something he was interested in. It wasn't a good idea for either of them. At least not now. It would bring unwanted attention and scrutiny. Her political opponents would have a field day. Mark's career would be contrasted with the crusading senator's politics. Worse, his family would be scrutinized and would lose their privacy. The twins would be the grandchildren of a sitting U.S. senator and would require additional security measures. Luci would receive unwanted attention. No, there would be no holiday weekends in the near future. Maybe someday.

Maybe soon. Luci sounded optimistic.

Mark had never been outright cold to her, but he had never warmed to her very much either. She suspected Luci's influence behind his semi-regular calls or texts. Early on, they had had a handful of deep discussions that needed to happen, but most of their interactions since then had felt, if not quite emotionless, certainly sterile.

She joked to herself that he kept in closer touch with her security detail than with her. Technically, that was true. Mark had insisted on making major adjustments to her personal security detail from day one—there were too many gaping holes. It was non-negotiable. Not even something he would discuss. Why had she uncharacteristically demurred so easily on the topic? Had she sensed in advance that their relationship would be lukewarm at best and she had better take anything she could get? Did it, in some strange way, make her feel cared for? At least it was a regular connection.

Luci had been much more familial, sending the senator occasional pictures and news about the adorable grandkids, whom she had seen on only two occasions when she happened to be in Massachusetts. Both times were at Luci's behest and were arranged as part of private meet-and-greets with the senator after local speaking engagements. McDermott remembered how her legs had gone weak when the Landrys entered the room the first time. She couldn't resist the desire to kneel down and hug the kids every chance she could during their short visit. She remembered holding them closely and how good they smelled.

She stared down at the phone in her hand and felt like a fool. What was she thinking? Mark was not going to just suddenly change his mind and invite her over to spend the long weekend with his family. It wasn't going to happen. It may never happen.

I'd settle for a text. As long as I knew the letters and numbers I was looking at were somehow connected to him, to those kids, to all of them.

She heard the doors open and felt a cold breeze followed by a familiar voice.

"You know, many of our senatorial colleagues seem to go to great lengths to accidentally bump into me so they can shore up support for their pet projects. You are one of the few who seem to go out of their way not to bump into me. I was starting to take it personally, Lois."

McDermott slipped the phone into the pocket of her long down coat and started to pull her gloves on. "Senator Johnson. You're looking vibrant for a man—"

"For what? A man of my age? Madam, I may have memorized the Gettysburg Address, but rumors that I attended are entirely false."

"I was going to say for a man who just stepped off a long plane ride. And no, I'm not intentionally avoiding you. You know better than that," she said, acknowledging their relationship dating back to her earliest days in the U.S. Senate, when he had been personally supportive and even mentor-like beyond the requirements of collegiality. He was a good and decent man.

She admired his respect for the institution and its traditions. He was steely, tempered, and impossible to rattle, all topped off with just enough Southern charm to not sound hokey. "Also, unlike many of my colleagues, my 'pet projects'—as you call them—remain unchanged.

You know, basically the things you would never consider supporting anyway."

Johnson smiled widely and rested his hand on her shoulder. "Never say never, Madam. And all joking aside, please be careful next week. When I heard about the trip, I didn't bother trying to talk you out of it. You're a big girl and can make your own decisions. But please be careful. It's dangerous for anybody and you are not just anybody. A Senate seat by definition makes you an extremely high-value target. Do what you have to do and get home safely, you hear? When you get back, you can tell Georgina all about it. She's been asking about you and looking for an excuse to have you over for dinner anyway."

She gently patted his hand through the soft calfskin glove on her shoulder. "Don't you worry about me, Senator. I'll be back before anyone even knows I was there and I'll be in good hands the whole time. And tell Georgina that if she ever wants to speak to me, she can call me directly—none of this 'going through the staff' thing for her."

"Will do. And since you have so graciously decided to meet with Judge James Midas next week, I no longer have to harass you on that particular topic. Thank you for taking the meeting. Even if it is off the books."

"I'm just meeting with him, Senator. And since you already know how I feel about his fitness for SCOTUS, I hope you don't have your hopes up. It's just a courtesy. You and I know the President is going to have to appoint someone else. The sooner he does, the sooner we can all move on. James Midas is never going to be confirmed."

"Never say never. Have a good evening, Lois. Give my warmest regards to your family."

She pulled on her gloves and exited the building to a waiting vehicle. Then she fastened her seatbelt and nodded to the driver. In turn, he informed the lead and trail security vehicles that they were ready to depart.

She resisted the urge to check her phone again. She knew there would be no new messages. At least not from Mark. Instead, she looked out the window at the passing D.C. scenery and rode home to her empty apartment in silence.

...

"Call Mark," Luci said to her automated system after pulling onto I-495 north and maneuvering her way into the far left lane. He answered after the second ring.

"Lady, I told you I was married so please stop calling me. My wife is a very jealous and dangerous woman."

"Very funny. I'm on my way home."

"How was your ride-along?"

"My last. I'm so done with this. The sooner I retire, the better. How are the babies?"

"Babies? There are no babies in this house. If you're referring to the big boy Carlos and the big girl named Amanda, they are fast asleep."

Luci smiled and checked her rear-view mirror.

"Good. I'll give them kisses when I get home. And if you play your cards right you may get one too."

"Sounds good to me."

"So, did you see the magazine? I left it in my office," she asked.

"What magazine?"

After several seconds of silence she shook her head, slightly annoyed. "You're a comedian tonight. Fine. See you later. Love you, babe."

"Drive safely. Love you too."

Mark retrieved his laptop and a warm bottle of champagne from the basement and returned to the kitchen. He placed the bottle in the freezer and fired up the laptop on the kitchen counter. Then he navigated his way to the archived security camera footage and clicked on a file marked "KEEPERS." Halfway down the list, he double-clicked on a file from two months ago and sat back with folded arms.

The video opened with a wide shot of the backyard. Amanda and Carlos could be seen playing on the jungle gym. He fast-forwarded several minutes to the part that had scared the hell out of him the first time he saw it. Two coyotes appeared on the edge of the screen where they halted and watched the kids for several moments. Unaware, the twins jumped and played in the backyard as the unwanted visitors then crept slowly toward them. Carlos noticed them first when they came within about twenty feet. He screamed and started to run, but Amanda grabbed him firmly around the wrist with one hand and held him still. Then she said something to him.

He froze in place. Amanda pointed her free hand at the coyotes and spoke to them directly. They paused for several seconds before continuing their slow creep closer to the kids. She shook her hand and spoke more forcefully, but the coyotes did not stop their advance.

Amanda Landry released her brother's wrist. Then she bent down and picked up a miniature baseball bat. Mark smiled and shook his head back and forth as his daughter held the weapon high above her head.

Here we go …

She screamed loudly and walked toward the coyotes at a deliberate pace while swinging the bat back and forth in front of her. The invaders froze momentarily before turning tail and darting into the woods. Amanda pursued until she was satisfied that they had fled.

Mark and Luci made two decisions that day. First, they fired the babysitter who had been inside the house video-chatting with her boyfriend instead of watching the kids. Second, Mark never took Murphy running with him again when the twins were home. He emailed a copy of the video to Luci and attached a note.

"Luci, take this to parent-teacher conferences next week."

He closed the laptop, separated the snail mail into two piles, and then walked into Luci's office on the main floor and dropped one of the piles on her desk. The room was immaculate and dust-free, with everything in its proper place. He gazed at the glass-encased map of Massachusetts mounted on the wall and squinted at the dozens of marks and notes she had made with multicolor erasable pens. Mark stepped back and smiled.

She has one hell of a work ethic. That's for sure.

A voice from upstairs broke his concentration. It was Carlos.

"Daddy! Daddy! Come please!"

...

Mark sat on the side of the bed and softly rubbed Carlos's back to calm him.

"What's wrong, little man?"

"There's a dragon in my closet, Daddy."

Mark nodded his head and scanned the dimly lit room. The only light was a blue glow coming from a Disney nightlight in the corner. He smiled and bent down to kiss his son on the back of his head.

"Are you sure? I've told you before that mommy and I specifically told the builder that this house was to be dragon-free. And so far, it has been. Do you want me to check just to make sure?"

Carlos looked up and nodded his head. "Yes, please."

"Okay," replied Mark. "But maybe I should ask Mandy to come in here and help us. Is that a good idea?"

"No, Daddy! Let her sleep. You check."

"I see," said Mark as he leaned down and whispered quietly into Carlos's ear. "She's in the closet, isn't she?"

The boy giggled and nodded his head.

Mark stood up, stuffed his hands into his front pockets, and started whistling softly. After a few seconds he slowly paced toward the closet and spoke loudly over his shoulder. "Okay, Carlos. I'll take a look. But I'm telling you there's no dragon in your closet."

When he twisted the knob and pulled open the closet door Amanda stepped out and screamed with both hands held over her head like gigantic dragon claws.

"Aaaahhhhh!"

Mark clutched his heart with both hands and staggered backwards for several steps.

"Oh my God, there really is a dragon in your closet!"

He collapsed to the floor and lay face down motionless. Amanda pounced on his back and immediately began to pinch, tickle, and push her father. Carlos joined in as soon as he could get off his bed. Mark tolerated it without reacting for as long as he could before erupting in laughter, rising to his knees, and eventually trapping a kid under each arm. He stood up and walked across the room.

"You guys are growing so fast. Remind me to add a few more pounds to my workout sandbags," he said as he dropped Carlos onto his bed with a thud. "Okay, you had your laugh. Mission accomplished. Good teamwork. Now go back to bed. I'll put the dragon back in her room. Good night, buddy. I love you."

"Love you too, Daddy."

. . .

"Will you put a few more drops of that in here, Mark?" Luci said, pointing to the nearly empty champagne flute on the kitchen table without taking her eyes off her laptop.

Mark fingered a few buttons on his smartphone and the kitchen speakers began playing Don Henley's "The Boys of Summer." The familiar synthetic drumbeat and slow-bending guitar notes made his wife smile. He was setting the mood.

Nobody on the road,
Nobody on the beach.
I feel it in the air,
The summer's out of reach.
Empty lake, empty streets,
The sun goes down alone.
I'm driving by your house
Don't know you're not home.

He approached her from behind and kissed her gently on the back of the head before reaching around with the bottle and filling her glass. He poured slowly and hummed along with the lyrics in her ear.

But I can see you,
Your brown skin shining in the sun.
You got your hair combed back
And your sunglasses on, baby.
I can tell you my love for you will still be strong
After the boys of summer have gone.

When she brought the crystal glass to her lips, he put the bottle down and switched his focus to her other ear, then stroked her tense neck and shoulders with his warm hands.

I never will forget those nights.
I wonder if it was a dream.
Remember how you made me crazy,
Remember how I made you scream.
I don't understand what happened to our love.
But, baby, I'm gonna get you back,
I'm gonna show you what I'm made of.

Mark rubbed himself against her back. Luci poured a large sip of champagne into her mouth and swished it around slowly with her tongue for a few seconds before swallowing. Working the mouse on her laptop with one hand, she reached behind with the other arm and gently slipped her fingers through the fly in Mark's boxers. "I see someone's ready to go. Can you hold that thought for a little while longer, babe? I just have to do a few quick things and then I'm all yours."

He backed away from her chair and turned the music down a notch. "Yup. Just remember I'll be in D.C. for a few days so you'll want to take advantage of me while you can." He emptied the bottle into his glass and picked up his smartphone to scroll through his notifications.

Luci broke the silence a few minutes later. "I spoke to your mother yesterday."

Mark looked up, expressionless. "Sorry, who?"

"Your mother. McDermott. Don't be an asshole, you know exactly who I'm talking about."

"Is she ready for her trip next week?"

"She didn't say much about that. Just that she is anxious and nervous at the same time. Anxious to see things up close with her own eyes. But nervous about what, if anything, she can do about it." Luci spun her chair around to face Mark. "She also mentioned that she hasn't thought about security once because she knows how hands-on you've been. She really appreciates it. But we spent most of the time talking about the kids and my post-retirement options. She gives good advice, you know."

"I'm sure she does."

"You know, Mark, I don't fully understand why you try to be as distant as you are to her. We've never tried to tell each other what to do and I'm not about to change that, but one day you might want to consider letting up a little bit. Not a lot. Just a little bit and go from there. We don't have any other family, Mark. It's just us and the kids. And she has nobody close to her since Megan left. And she won't be around forever."

"I told you I would."

"Well, you've been saying that for a long time. One day it'll be too late. And by the way, what will your kids think if you don't tell them until they're older? When they ask why you denied them a grandmother when it mattered most—during their childhood—will you have a good enough answer? If not, maybe it's time. That's it. I'm done. I won't say another word."

"Yeah, right. For how long?"

"You're in D.C. again soon. If you called or even just texted to say hello for no particular reason, I know it would mean the world to her. Just consider it. That's all."

"Will do." Although he tried to suppress them, the only images he had ever seen of his father flashed in his mind. Newspaper images of a young man standing by a helicopter. A boot camp graduation photo. A flag-covered casket. Luci's voice broke the trance.

"You act like you don't really care, but you sure spend a lot of time worrying about her safety. And don't tell me it's because she's some kind of client. There's more there."

"Catholic guilt."

"Bullshit. You care because she's your mother. You care. But don't worry, I won't make you say it."

She was right. Mark did feel a natural instinct to protect McDermott; after all, Lois McDermott was his mother. And although Mark didn't care much for her politics—or any politics, for that matter—he did not lack legitimate affection for her. He respected her strength and resiliency. She had gone through a series of crushing losses—public nightmares that had robbed her of some of the most precious things in her life—yet she continued to soldier on. Still, he could never shake the feeling that she had something to hide. But he never let it bother him too much. How could he? There were plenty of things about himself that he would never share with her. He had his reasons. She must have hers.

Mark held the magazine open in front of him and alternated his gaze between the pages and his wife. "Hey, are you Detective Lieutenant Luci Landry?"

"Yes, I am." She bit down gently and held a scrunchie with her teeth while she worked her long black hair into a ponytail with her hands.

"One of *Boston Globe Magazine*'s 'Women to Watch' in Massachusetts? That Luci Landry?"

"That's me."

Mark cleared his throat and began reading aloud. " 'She is perhaps one of a few LEOs with statewide name recognition. ... Smart, tough, resilient ... these are just a few of the words used to describe Landry by her peers and superiors ... yada yada yada ... handpicked for the Governor's task force on women and children ... yada yada yada ... She is married to Mark Landry, a private security executive with Boston-based Imperium, and has twin five-year-old children.' This is great. Has it kicked up any post-retirement offers yet?"

"Yeah. But nothing that makes me want to jump out of my seat. I don't want to accept something just for the sake of accepting it. It's not like we need the money. I don't want something that makes me say yes. I'm holding out for a 'hell yes.'"

"It'll come. But as good as this piece is, they left out the most important part."

Luci saved her document and closed the lid of her laptop. "What did they miss?"

He looked again at the full-color glossy photo of Luci in her dress blue uniform with the American and Massachusetts flags as a backdrop. "That you're even hotter in real life." He tossed the magazine onto the counter and dimmed all the lights until the room was almost in complete darkness. Then he slowly brought up the brightness of a single kitchen spotlight mounted directly over Luci's chair. She held her empty flute in the air and softly wiggled it back and forth, indicating that she wanted more.

"There's no more champagne. But I'll share the rest of mine with you." Mark retrieved his drink and walked slowly toward her. He patted his growing bulge and looked at her with the most innocent, sympathy-invoking eyes he could muster. "Seriously, I'm about to die."

"Get over here, then. We can't have you dying on us."

Mark handed her the glass and pulled his boxers down to just above his knees. She took a long, slow sip of champagne with one hand and slowly stroked him with the other.

His breathing became shallower.

She poured the rest of the champagne into her mouth and swished it around with her tongue. Once it was warm, she let it spill from her lips onto her working hand and looked up at him with that mischievous smile she got whenever she was in control. He moaned as his legs got weaker.

"I've been thinking about this all day. Do—Not—Stop."

When she took him into her mouth, he inhaled sharply, steadied himself on the back of her chair with one hand, and gently grasped her ponytail with the other. He looked down into her eyes.

This is not going to take long.

CHAPTER TWO: Imperium

"Task, conditions, and standards, Kenny. You know what they are. One round in the chest. From full concealment this time. As soon as you hear the beep. One round in the chest. Aim for dead center. Try not to think about it so much this time. Just get the gun out of concealment and put a round in the center of the target as fast as you possibly can. I know you can do this. It's all about efficiency. It's not about doing everything as fast as you can—it's about saving time by only doing what's absolutely necessary. Economy of effort, right? That means don't do anything unless it's absolutely necessary. Actions require time, and depending on the circumstances, you probably won't have much. I'm talking fractions of a second. Got it? You ready?"

Kenny let his arms dangle loosely at his sides and nodded his head.

"One round in the chest. On the beep. Stand by ..."

Mark pressed a button on the handheld shot timer and held it up behind Kenny's head at ear level. After several seconds, a loud digital beep broke the silence to inform Kenny that the clock was ticking and would not stop until the timer's audio sensors detected his gunshot.

Upon hearing the beep, Kenny immediately grabbed the front tails of his untucked shirt with both hands and pulled the garment to chest level. Then he snapped his right hand downward and firmly gripped the .380 holstered inside his belt in the appendix position. He drew the gun and gripped it with both hands as he quickly oriented his sights and pulled the trigger. The round hit the top portion of the target's shoulder.

"It's a hit. Better than a miss. But don't sacrifice accuracy for speed. Look for a balance between the two. Regardless, the time isn't bad at all when we consider where you started."

He held up the shot timer and pointed to Kenny's time.

"Better. Still nowhere near your kind of time."

"Kenny. Trust me, you've come a long way. I used to be able to time you with a calendar."

Kenny laughed as Mark quickly checked a message that had just come through on his phone. He laughed but inside he was still frustrated with his average performance. Kenny looked up to all the operators, but especially Mark, Billy, Max, and Sadie. They were Dunbar and Mark's inner circle. The best of the best. The go-to team for anything and everything. Mark didn't understand how badly Kenny wanted to be respected by them. And Kenny didn't understand that they respected him already.

"I gotta get upstairs. I have a bunch of things to do before I head to D.C. Remember, we have a new guy coming on today and I want to get him on-boarded quickly. That means smart earbuds, glasses, and phone ASAP."

"Got it. It's all ready for him. I'll walk him through all the bells and whistles myself."

"Perfect. On a different note, NSA has a few things for you to look at this week. Equation Group, I think. Can't remember. I'll send you the info I have." Mark finished his sentence and waited for the anticipated wince, then pointed at Kenny's face. "I knew that face was coming."

Kenny's relationship with the NSA—mostly due to his own rebellious attitude—had been bumpy, especially during his early days working for Dunbar and Mark. The unpleasantness that had defined his early interactions with the agency had mostly dissipated, but tensions lingered, no doubt fueled by Kenny's past as a hacker. Hackers are not monolithic, but many share a disdain for authority—especially government authority. The diehard hacking community would see walking into NSA HQ at Fort Meade as akin to Frodo walking into Mordor and tossing the ring over to Sauron instead of destroying it. Kenny hadn't felt quite that bad about joining the former enemy, but he did still have some trust issues. As a result, he had kept NSA people at arm's distance from his work whenever possible as a precaution—a decision fully supported by Mark and Dunbar, who shared a healthy skepticism for anyone outside Imperium.

"Nah, no worries. They're not that bad. I'll make sure I'm available."

"Good. One more thing on NSA," he said smiling. "Patricia Johnson—I believe you know her as Patty—will be in town for a few days. She has some kind of egghead meetings with MIT Media Lab, iRobot, Natick Labs, the usual rounds. I'll let her share the details. She wants your opinion on some things and hopes you'll have time. Since I assumed you are still in love with her, I said you were available."

Mark paused until Kenny displayed an ear-to-ear grin. "I knew that face was coming too. I'll see you later. Billy's back from Belgium and waiting for me upstairs."

Mark turned to leave the underground range and return to his office on the third floor of the building. Kenny called out from behind him, still holding the shot timer.

"Mark, wait. Before you leave. Your turn. Let's see what you got."

"Fine."

He walked back to the firing line, bowed his head, and let his arms dangle freely at his sides. Kenny approached from behind and both men waited for the beep.

By the time Kenny recognized the familiar sound, Mark had already cleared his shirt out of the way and drawn the Heckler and Koch VP9 from his appendix holster. Two quick trigger presses later, he returned the gun to its holster and headed toward his office.

Kenny looked up and saw that both rounds had landed within millimeters of each other, between the target's eyes. Then he looked at the shot timer to see how long the drill had taken.

"Jesus. Is that even possible?"

...

Imperium's offices and facilities were housed in an unremarkable, square brick building a few blocks' walk from the Long Wharf area of Boston. When the elevators opened on the third floor, Mark stepped into a rectangular room and waited for the elevators to close behind him before engaging the main door's keypad.

The 24-hour operations center—commonly referred to by Imperium employees as the Game Room—was humming with activity. Although the private security company was based in Boston, its tentacles reached around the globe. With roughly two hundred employees and trusted adjuncts, including 32 (soon to be 33) high-level tactical operators, Imperium could task and support multiple direct action operations in support of its clients' needs.

Some of the operators were former Family operators who went with Dunbar after the unit was terminated and he founded Imperium. Others came from various military and law enforcement organizations. They had been chosen for their combination of proven track records under pressure and their ability to work under the harshest of circumstances. They also had some of the most experienced minds in the cyber world, many of whom, like Kenny, had checkered pasts.

Mark had already retired when the Family was officially disbanded. When that happened, Dunbar started Imperium almost immediately and squeezed every last resource he could to create a private company with as many of the same capabilities as the Family as he could recreate. Then he nailed down contracts with a short list of exclusive customers, including the U.S. government, and had the company fully operational in almost no time. All the while, Dunbar still had his fingers crossed, hoping that the bureaucrats and do-gooders in Washington would see the error of their ways and recommission his special unit. But his optimism had been running on fumes for the past year or two, and Dunbar had slowly been pulling away. He was still the final word at Imperium, but for all intents and purposes Mark had taken control of operations and daily management.

Billy was sitting on the sofa beside Mark's desk, cleaning a small semiautomatic pistol with a sour look on his face. Mark stopped in the doorway and smiled. "Welcome back, Brother. Good to see you've chosen my office as your litter box," he said, pointing to the gun solvent, Q-tips, and gun parts on the coffee table.

"You keep saying it's your office but all I see is Dunbar's stuff," he answered, gesturing to the walls where pictures, newspaper clippings, and other wall hangings underscored the highlights of Dunbar's career.

In one picture, Dunbar wore tiger-stripe fatigues while posing with two men almost half his height somewhere deep in the jungle of Vietnam. In the next display, a Colombian newspaper celebrated the death of cocaine kingpin Pablo Escobar. Below the headline was a picture of a half-dozen Colombian soldiers with rifles and ear-to-ear smiles, posing with Escobar's dead body on a rooftop as if they had been his executioners. There was a framed Polaroid of Panamanian President Manuel Noriega crying like a little girl after his capture. The fall of the Berlin Wall, the collapse of the Soviet Union, the global war on terror—Dunbar had been an active player in some of the most significant moments in contemporary black ops history. He was a true legend.

"I'll tell you what. You stay right there and be me for a few days. We currently have two EP teams in the field. One in Singapore and one in Panama City. We also have ghost teams in Dearborn and Miami. And about two dozen cyber-operators are busy here 24/7, doing God only knows what. Have fun. I'll go be you. We'll see how you feel in a few days."

Billy acted as if he was thinking about it for a few seconds. " 'Uneasy lies the head that wears a crown.' No thanks." He gathered his things and stood up. "Have a seat, Boss. I'll follow you anywhere."

"That's what I thought. Tell me about Belgium. Did you bring the witness video of the last raid? I haven't seen it yet."

"Yeah." Billy pulled the beat-up Oklahoma Sooners cap from his back pocket and popped it on his head. Then he touched the widescreen display in Mark's office and queued up a video. "So I gotta say, overall, they weren't bad at all. The boys know their stuff. But damn, at the beginning of the week I told them it was a bad idea to notify local precincts that they would be conducting raids in the area. They ignored me, so we spent the better part of the week raiding empty hooches, two of which were friggin' booby-trapped."

Mark moved some things around on his desk and punched a few of the keys on his desktop. "Keep going. I'm listening."

"Finally they got the picture that it's a bad idea to broadcast your ops. Not because the cops will tell the bad guys, but because the cops and admin will tell their friends and families to stay away from those areas and shit will spread from there. There must be no Dutch, or French, or German, or friggin' Flemish word for OPSEC. But anyway, I digress. Here's the final raid where we took lemons and made lemonade. Some bystander's cellphone footage. You'll appreciate this, Mark. When you watch it, think about what we did back in Kosovo."

The cellphone video opened with a narrow view of marked and unmarked police cars parked in front of a congested apartment building in Leuven, Belgium, just east of Brussels. Nine operators attached to the Veiligheid van de Staat—the Belgian state security services—enter a first-floor apartment. A single shot rings out. The small crowd outside gasps. After five tense minutes, the officials exit with a cuffed, hooded, kicking-and-screaming prisoner in tow. He is dragged into the back of an SUV and the caravan departs. The screen goes dark.

"End scene," said Billy in his best director's voice with one hand in the air. "What'd you think?"

"Nicely done."

"Would you have known if I hadn't mentioned Kosovo?"

"Maybe." He pointed at the screen. "I saw nine guys go in and nine guys come out, including the prisoner. Then everyone drove away. Which means there was probably nobody inside, so you had one of the guys play the prisoner role just to freak out the rest of their network. Not sure if I would have noticed if you hadn't prepped me though."

"Bullshit. You're Mark Landry—you don't miss details. Collecting dots is easy; connecting them is the hard part. You would have noticed. Regardless, being the corporate-minded company man that you are now, I am sure you will want to know that the only round discharged during the operation was liberated from my Glock into a jam-packed bookcase. No humans or animals were harmed. I even picked up my shell casing. Be sure to mention that in the environmental impact section of your report to the Belgian government."

"Any subsequent movement?"

"Yeah. Lots of confusion. Jihadis expected to watch us hit empty apartment after empty apartment. When this video hit the web, there was a huge spike in local chatter and movement. They don't know what the hell to think. They know they got their guys out before the raid, but the footage has them second-guessing everything. They're getting nervous and will inevitably do something stupid—assuming the good guys are smart enough to keep their mouths shut and not blow it."

"When are you headed back?"

"Not for a month or two. So you're stuck with me for a while."

"Good. I need you here. Lots going on." Mark paused, flipping through the papers on his desk. "Seriously, Billy. I need you around."

"No worries, man. I got nowhere else to be. Why? What's up?"

"Nothing specific. Just lots going on and perhaps some opportunities. I meet with Dunbar tomorrow and he's hinting at an important conversation. This could be the big one, but lately you never know with Dunbar.

"You mean reforming The Family?"

"No idea. Beyond that, there's a new guy coming on today. You liked him and recommended him during selection, so I assume you'll be cool with having him shadow you for a while."

"Yeah, man. The local guy, right?"

"Yeah." Mark located the new guy's bio and pulled it from the stack in his in-box. The top of the page read *Operator #33*. Mark skimmed the highlights.

David Ferreira. Parents emigrated to the U.S. from the Portuguese Azores. Born in Fall River, Massachusetts in 1975. Large family who worked mainly in the now-dried-up Massachusetts textile industry or as fishermen. Four years of active duty service in the United States Marine Corps as a 2336 Explosive Ordnance Disposal (EOD) technician. Attended community college and the Massachusetts State Police Academy. Twenty-plus years on the job. SWAT leader, experienced cold-weather Divemaster, multiple joint task forces. Licensed pilot.

"Here's his sheet. Good guy. An excellent fit. Consider him deployable anywhere as of right now. Oh, and he knows Boston and Massachusetts like the back of his hand. Can I count on you to help get him up and running? Give him the standard brief: 'Welcome. Great to have you. You made it through a lot to be here but keep in mind that selection ...'"

Billy cut him off. "Selection is an ongoing process."

"Exactly."

"Will do. I'll let you get some work done and catch you later."

"One more thing," Mark called out. "Kenny's NSA crush will be in town for a few days and he no doubt plans on wooing her. Do me a favor—take the new guy, David, and keep an eye on them when she's here, okay? Don't let him know—he'd be pissed. But she's a valuable NSA asset and important client so I don't want to take any chances. We have no reason to be worried, but I want to be safe and it's a good opportunity for you to get the new guy's feet wet. Not that he'll learn anything about Boston from an Okie like you."

"Okie? I prefer Sooner American."

An Imperium analyst knocked twice on the door as he entered. "Pardon me. This is the complete plan for Senator McDermott's trip." He dropped a file on Mark's desk and exited. Mark looked at the file and then at Billy.

"I'll catch you later, thanks."

He turned on cable news and read the headline across the bottom of the screen: *Supreme Court Vacancy Reaches 200th Day—U.S. Senate Deadlocked.* He muted the volume and turned his attention to McDermott's plan, reviewing it for what seemed like the hundredth time and making sure that attention had been paid to the tiniest details. Primary and backup transportation options, communications plan, protective intelligence summaries for the different locations she'd be visiting, emergency medical contingencies, an emergency supply of the Senator's blood type, and an appropriate supply of any necessary prescriptions. Everything looked good, but he would continue to review it up to departure. The stakes were too high to make a mistake.

A sitting U.S. Senator is a high-value target for America's enemies, and traveling abroad was always risky—especially where she was going. But she was also Mark's only living parent and he felt a moral obligation to protect her. He tossed the file onto his desk and stroked a few keys on his computer. The image of a forty-five-year-old newspaper clipping appeared on the wall screen.

"Four Perish in Fort Drum Helicopter Crash," read the headline. Beneath it was a large photo of four men standing next to a UH1-Huey helicopter. A mechanical failure had caused the pilot to lose control of the aircraft and crash into an open field. All four men were killed on impact. The man on the far right was Mark's biological father, Theodore "Teddy" Cartwright. He had been at Fort Drum for only a few months when he met Mark's then seventeen-year-old mother. Young and confused, she had been waiting for the right time to tell him of the pregnancy when he was killed. He was nineteen years old.

Mark looked at the clipping and compared it to Teddy's official Department of the Army photo, taken at the completion of basic training. He could not recall a single time in his entire life when he had felt sad or depressed about not knowing who his parents were. Why? It wasn't something he could control. Besides, he had never wanted for anything. Agnes and Father Peck had been more than any kid could have asked for. Yet he couldn't help but notice the tinge of melancholy he felt whenever he thought of Teddy.

Poor guy. So young.

He opened McDermott's security plan again and spent several minutes going back and forth between it and Teddy's records.

I wonder what they looked like together. What they saw in each other. If she laughed at his jokes. If he was as good to her as McDermott says.

He checked the time and needed to move on, but something was nagging him about McDermott's travel security plan. He made a mental note to check it again later and have Billy take a look as well. Right now, he had to check in with ongoing ops and prepare for D.C. Dunbar had some sort of news and Mark was curious as to what it might be.

Is POTUS poised to recommission the Family? That had always been Dunbar's hope. It had always been Mark's hope too – with himself at the helm.

Or does Dunbar simply want to talk about clients? Whatever it was, Mark was looking forward to the conversation. Life was good and money was great, but part of him still had much bigger ambitions. And nobody thought bigger than Dunbar.

Yes, he was looking forward to this meeting. And it was good timing, because things were relatively quiet in the Boston office right now. Mark prioritized what he needed to accomplish before leaving, shut his office door, and got to work.

. . .

"We'll have another round whenever you get the chance. No rush," Kenny told the waitress as she cleared the plates from the table. Patty was watching an instant replay from the Bruins game on the Harp's wide screen. A crushing hip-check sent a rival player against the boards so hard his fillings might have come loose. The crowd in the pub cheered and banged their fists on the bar. Patty smiled and cheered along as Kenny stared at her. She sensed his gaze and winked at him out of the corner of her eye.

Stunning. That's what you are. Abso-friggin-lutely stunning. The whole package. Just the way I like'em. Smart as hell; curvy and thick; dimples so big I could fall into them when you smile. I would drink your bathwater.

"This will be over soon," Kenny said pointing at the screen. "And although that was a fantastic hit, we're about to lose. That means a gazillion pissed-off Bruins fans are about to flow out of the Garden, which is about one hundred feet from where we sit."

"Yeah, let's not be here when that happens. Finish these last drinks and go somewhere else then?" she asked.

"Definitely. I know a bunch of cool spots not far from my place."

"Sounds good. Now that I can hear again, finish your thought for me. You were talking about attribution, right?"

"Yeah, like I was saying. The whole debate is a smokescreen. Purely political. You know that. Attribution is not one hundred percent possible one hundred percent of the time, but it usually is. And it was never a problem before, when governments just wanted to arrest individual hackers. In those cases, we were always able to trace things right to the bad guy's apartment. That all changed once states started playing around in cyberspace. Now all of a sudden, people think attribution is impossible. You and I both know it's not."

Kenny paused to choose his next words very carefully, because he never knew who might be listening.

"You and I both know that it's not only possible but very likely that most attacks can be attributed most of the time. And this task is much easier for our side because we control some of the Internet's critical infrastructure."

Patty smiled and took a sip of her Long Island iced tea. He continued talking. She pretended to listen but had other things on her mind.

You have no idea how adorable you are. Do you, Kenny? Usually not my type but, man, what is it about this guy?

"Enough on that stuff, though. I'm not telling you anything you don't already know. Let's get back to you. Your undergrad degree is in sociology or something, but where'd you get your technical chops?"

Patty lowered her drink to the table gently and leaned back in her seat.

"Since both my parents earned their degrees at Howard, I didn't have much of a choice where to go to school. Thankfully, I did get to choose my own courses so I majored in sociology. But my roommate was a computer science major, and I got bit by the bug and nerded out on my own. I learned by setting up my own honeypots and sandboxes, seeing what popped in to say hello—all for fun. Then I messed around with Backtrack, Netstat and IDA Pro, you know, just to take the binaries apart and stuff like that and see what they were doing. When my employer came to Howard's campus to recruit, I got in line and ended up getting hired. I've been there for nine years and a team leader for the past three, and I love it."

An eruption of groans in the bar announced the end of the hockey game across the street.

"That's our warning," said Kenny. "The angry horde will be here soon. Want to go somewhere else?"

She nodded her head and weighed her options.

Is he ever going to make a move or are we just going to hop from place to place? I know he's interested—he's looking at me like I'm lunch. But we've been here before and he never closes the deal. Should I just take him by the hand? Maybe he's scared or inexperienced.

"I have an idea, Kenny. Let's just skip the next pub and go hang out at your place."

Kenny froze like a deer in the headlights. He liked the idea and wanted to voice his support but struggled to find the words.

"Um, yeah. Yeah."

"You don't sound very excited," Patty said as she stretched out her arm and gently grabbed his hand. Kenny's heart rate soared.

"No. Yeah. Definitely. Believe me, I'm excited. Let's get the hell out of here."

...

Patty wrapped both of her arms around one of Kenny's and gave him a peck on the cheek. "Can you feel how cold my nose is?"

"Oh, yeah. Don't worry, you'll be nice and warm again soon. It's not a long walk."

Traffic cops kept order as cars spilled from parking garages and throngs of people dispersed from the Garden in various stages of inebriation.

"Why are some of them chanting 'Yankees suck!' at a hockey game? That doesn't make sense."

"Really? Makes perfect sense to me. You mean they don't do that everywhere?"

She laughed. "Not in Atlanta."

With warm smiles on their faces they held hands and walked, barely noticing the eager, faster-paced crowd thickening around them. They turned right and continued straight for several blocks until a Boston cop held up his hands, asking all pedestrians to clear the crosswalk so he could let a long waiting line of cars exit the area. Patty was telling Kenny a story from her sorority days at Howard when an empty glass bottle suddenly shattered at their feet. Thankfully, it had been wrapped in a paper bag by whoever had drained it of its contents. The bag had kept the glass from flying, but the sound was enough to startle those nearby.

"Where the hell did that come from? Stick close together in case we have to get out of here quickly." He grasped her hand firmly and pulled her closer. Then he began scanning the crowd on the opposite side of the street as best he could between the passing cars.

He scanned left to right, then back and forth several times before his attention was naturally drawn to a tall man at Kenny's ten o'clock position. He seemed to be staring, pointing, and yelling directly at them. Kenny spoke to Patty without taking his eyes off the man.

"Do you see that guy across the street at ten o'clock?"

"Yeah, I think he threw whatever that was and he's staring at me."

"Do you know him?"

"No! Never seen him in my life. Maybe he wasn't aiming for us."

"I don't know about that. I don't have my glasses on, but it seems like he's looking right at us. It's time to cross. Just keep walking and stay close."

Halfway across the street, Kenny approached two traffic cops and pointed to the man. "Gentlemen, that guy just threw a bottle or something into the crowd. No idea who he is. Drunk. Maybe crazy. Just letting you know." Then he continued walking.

Patty looked back over her shoulder to see one of the officers point to the man and blow his whistle. "Hey, blue hat. Don't go anywhere. Wait right there and talk to me for a moment, please." He held up his hands as the man began to protest. "Yeah, yeah, yeah. Just a quick question and you'll be on your way, chief."

"Thank God. The police are grabbing him. What a nutjob!"

"Keep moving. Let's just get some distance between us and him. The cops have bigger things to worry about. Unless he acts like a complete jackass with them, they'll probably just chew his ass and hold him up for a few minutes. Let's not be around when they let him go."

They crossed another narrow street and turned left. The crowd thinned as they walked. Kenny recalled Mark and Billy's advice about keeping your strong hand free to be ready to defend yourself.

"Let's switch sides."

He released his grasp on Patty's hand and guided her to his left side, freeing his right. After another block he checked behind them again and then slowed their pace. The snow started to come down heavier. Patty opened her mouth wide and tried to catch a few snowflakes with her tongue.

"Okay. I feel better. We're good. Are you still hungry? I don't have much at my place, but we can stop on the way to get anything you want."

"Do you have something to use as a nightcap and an extra toothbrush?"

Kenny stopped walking and faced her. His mind scrambling for a reply that wouldn't telegraph his excitement about what he thought was coming. Patty moved closed and put her arms on his shoulders.

Are you gonna kiss me or what? You're into me, right? Unless I've completely misread you. How many more signals do you need, Kenny? Why so timid with me? What is it? Maybe he's just never been with a black woman before or something.

Kenny tilted his head to the side and leaned in close. Gently, he kissed her on the lips. Then he pulled away.

"Get back over here and do that again," she ordered playfully.

Kenny tilted his head in the opposite direction and did it again. Patty swooned and ran one hand through the hair on the back of his head while she twirled the tip of her tongue around the inside of Kenny's mouth. He marveled at their reflection in the dimly lit window of the store behind her and felt prouder than he could remember. There they were, together at last, as the snow fell gently around them. He reached around and grabbed her rear end with both hands.

This is the best moment of my life.

The fist, elbow, or whatever it was connected with the right side of Kenny's head and sent him tumbling to the sidewalk, flickering on the edge of consciousness for several seconds. He struggled to gain some sort of footing, but the sucker-punch-on-steroids had short-circuited his nervous system. He did not know what was happening.

He felt several blows to his body. Punches or kicks or something, he assumed.

Then he heard Patty's bloodcurdling screams for help. Then the beating stopped. Then Patty's screaming stopped. Then the blows began anew. Kenny's mind raced for a problem to solve.

Then it stopped again.

Kenny rolled onto his back. Blood was flowing into his eyes from a wound on the top of his head. He struggled to focus on the figure standing over him. A dark figure wearing a hat. Now he could hear a different voice screaming from nearby.

I wonder where Patty is.

46

The voice got louder and louder. "No! Don't even think about it! Show me your fucking hands right now! Hands! Hands! Hands!"

Is that Billy? That sure sounds like Billy.

Kenny was seeing double vision, so he closed one eye and harnessed every ounce of energy he could muster into focusing the other eye on the threat. The man either did not hear or simply did not plan on following Billy's orders. He reached a hand into the inside breast pocket of his thick parka and removed something with a gloved hand.

Kenny fought to remain conscious, but the physical and psychological trauma was overloading his mind. He was fading quickly. He watched as the man held the large object in both hands and extended his arms toward Kenny. An extraordinary beam of green light leaped from his hands into Kenny's one good eye. It was the last thing he saw before shutting down completely. The last thing he heard was the gunshots.

...

Billy called Mark within seconds after notifying the authorities of what had transpired.

Mark walked into the Mass General Hospital ER shortly after Kenny arrived. The new guy, David, was standing outside the examining room, talking to two Boston cops. He ended his conversation and met Mark halfway.

"No changes. He's conscious. Coherent but groggy as hell. They're doing a CT and a bunch of other tests. He's got some other good bumps and bruises, but nothing's broken and no internal bleeding. I was talking with him before. He was pretty frantic but calmed right down once Patty was allowed in. He was more concerned with her than anything else."

Mark nodded but didn't reply.

David leaned in and looked Mark earnestly in the eyes. "I take responsibility for this. And I can't think of anything worse happening on my first day. I'll turn in my stuff as soon as I get back to the office."

Mark put his hand on David's shoulder. "Negative. You're not going anywhere. You're earned your spot. Trust me, we're going to look at this closely and fix it. But things could have been much worse. Remember that."

David nodded.

"Billy is taking care of things with the BPD and trying to get an ID on the attacker. All available video and photos from nearby security cameras are being reviewed as we speak. Police are interviewing witnesses but they're not telling us anything we don't already know. Some guy ambushed Kenny and Patty. We need to find out who he was and why. Tell Billy to meet me in the Game Room as soon as he finishes."

Patty looked up when Mark quietly pulled back the blue dividing curtain and entered Kenny's treatment area. He stood at the foot of the bed, looking at his friend and colleague. Patty noted the expression on his face but couldn't quite find the right words to describe it—a strange fusion of concern and rage that flashed so quickly she barely caught it. Mark, like Dunbar, was fiercely loyal to and protective of his people. In turn, both men received the same loyalty from their operators.

Mark approached her and gently rubbed her shoulder. "You doing okay, Patty? I just spoke with your boss. They're sending a few folks to come and take you back to D.C. safely. Just a precaution."

"I understand their concern, but I'm not going anywhere. I'm staying right here with Kenny."

Mark looked down at the bed. Kenny's left eye was dark purple and swollen almost completely shut. There were cuts and scrapes across his chin. He knew that he would find more if he looked under Kenny's hospital garment. Kenny groaned as he sat up straighter and looked at Patty.

"Hey. I have a feeling it looks worse than it is. Don't stay here on my account. I'll be fine."

She leaned in and whispered in his ear. "I don't care. I'm not leaving your side."

Mark pulled his phone from the front pocket of his leather jacket and glanced at it for a few seconds. "Okay, we can cross that bridge when we get to it. I know you've both been asked already, but do you have any idea who he might have been?"

"No, none at all," answered Patty. "He looked either mad as hell or straight-up crazy, but I've never seen him before in my life."

"I know it sounds easy, but try not think about it too much. You may have just been in the wrong place at the wrong time. Bad luck, perhaps. But considering your career paths, maybe not. For that reason, we need to err on the side of caution and keep both of you safe. Can I have a moment with Kenny, please?"

Patty kissed Kenny on the forehead and left for the restroom. "I'm sorry, Mark."

Mark moved to the side of the bed and put a hand on his forearm. "You're sorry? Kenny, please. You got ambushed in the street by a lunatic. You have nothing to be sorry about." He sat on the side of the bed and lowered his voice. "Listen, don't get mad at me for asking this, but it needs to be asked and you know that. You've known her for a while now. Have you ever been concerned about anything with her?"

"Mark. Some asshole just ambushed me for no reason. Maybe he lost money on a hockey game. But to answer your question—no."

"No? Never? Nothing? Not once did you ever get a weird feeling after she did or said something? Last time I'm going to ask. Just humor me and think it through again."

Kenny inhaled sharply and winced at the pain of his bruised ribs. "No. Never, Mark."

"Good enough for me." He stood and zipped his jacket. "David will be at your side until we find some things out. I'm going to get on that stuff right now. I want you to relax and do what the docs tell you to do."

"Wait. How about answering a question for me? What was Billy doing there?"

"You got very lucky, my friend. Billy just happened to be out getting the new guy, David, up to speed. He was showing him the ropes on how we do surveillance detection routes, tracking, counter-surveillance. They picked you guys up when the game let out and decided to stick with you for a few blocks for fun. Thank God for the timing."

Mark pulled out his phone and sent Dunbar a message.

MARK: Kenny ok … bell rung good/concussion … NSA girl uninjured … no motive or ID on suspect's body

DUNBAR: Roger … keep me informed … rely on your team to keep things going and keep your D.C. travel plans … we need to meet

MARK: Copy

…

Mark and Billy stood in front of the big screen in the Game Room with a small group of Imperium analysts and cyber-operators. Billy added narrative to the patchwork of images and video unfolding before them.

"David and I were with them all day. Multiple locations throughout the city. Zero issues, no detectible surveillance. All was well … until the hockey game let out and the streets filled with chuckleheads."

He identified a video in the upper right corner of the screen with the laser pointer.

"Expand that one, please. Thank you. Here you can see the threat standing on the curb across the street from the principals. Slow it down, please. Thank you. There he is. Nothing anomalous. He looks at his watch. He scratches his nuts. Taking in the crowd on the other side of the street when—boom!—he sees something or someone he doesn't like. Starts screaming something. We don't know what because these particular street cameras do not have audio. Grabs a bottle from the recycle bin on the corner and chucks it at Kenny and Patty. Two cops standing nearby. Lots of witnesses. No apparent motive."

Billy walked in front of the display and pointed at another video. "That one there, please. Thank you. Kenny does a smart thing here and lets the cops know they have a chucklehead on their hands. Then he exits the area. In this angle, you can see one of the cops approach him. You can also see David enter the frame and close distance with the threat. There is an exchange of words. No doubt he's telling the cop he has no idea who threw the bottle. Body language indicates agitation but he's not being disorderly. At this point we both peeled off and tried to get back in step with the principals, but the crowd was dense and growing."

Billy bowed his head and spoke to the analyst running the screen. "Put up the last one, please."

The video began with Kenny and Patty's kiss. Light foot traffic passes them by. Most pay them no particular attention. One young woman snaps a selfie with them. The attacker enters the frame in a flash and hits Kenny with an open fist, with enough force to make the room gasp.

Mark cringed and breathed deeply. He was standing stoically with his arms folded, but under the calm surface there was bubbling lava.

Seeing someone barbarically attack Kenny and then beat him when he was down was infuriating. Seeing him turn away from Kenny and slap Patty hard enough to send her flying was maddening. But seeing someone pull a gun and paint Kenny's forehead with a green laser pushed Mark to a level of rage he did not often reach. This rage could be placated only by the two rounds Billy deposited in the monster's head before he could pull his own trigger.

"Coroner and forensics folks are trying to ID him now. He had what appeared to be a brand-spanking-new Venezuelan passport. The only things he had on him were the weapon—a suppressed Springfield XDS 9mm equipped with a green laser—about two grand in cash, and a digital burner phone. I grabbed the phone and left everything else there for the locals. We can share information with them through back channels if we need to, but there was no way I was going to let it get tagged and entered into the abyss where we never get a crack at it. Our cyber-ops guys are giving it their best whack right now. I haven't heard anything yet on lifestyle chemicals found on the phone. But if anything comes up that may help us identify this guy—a rare cologne, traces of materials that might identify the industry he works in, things like that— I'll let you know. For now, he's a John Doe. Hopefully that won't last long. Mark?"

Mark nodded and breathed deeply. "I'm pissed. Actually, I'll be honest—this fucking enrages me." He pointed to the screen. "That is one of our own right there." Then he pointed down. "And this is our home base. Let's find out what the hell happened."

He turned to Billy, who picked up on Mark's comments. "Yeah, let's get cracking and find out who this asshole was. The odds that he was just some random idiot or drunk hockey fan dropped considerably when the tricked-out sidearm and encrypted burner phone entered the picture. But right now, all we have is questions. We need answers. Do whatever you have to do to get them."

Mark approached the screen and stood next to Billy, facing the rest of the team.

"We're not sure how many people at NSA or elsewhere had access to Patty's business here in town, but we're looking into it. Right now, nothing makes sense. Our job is to make sense of it and solve the problem. Let me know what you need from me and keep me informed."

Then he turned to address Billy separately. "I'm going home soon to pack my stuff. After I drop the kids at school, I'm going straight to D.C. to meet with Dunbar. Stay on top of this, okay? I'm counting on you."

Mark told an analyst to send several of the videos to the screen in his office. Billy followed behind him and closed the door.

"Hey, I'm heading back out to take a closer look at the passport and pistol this guy had on him. Also gonna talk to the Boston cops and see if they know anything else. Listen, I'm sorry. I was in charge and I dropped the ball. I thought we were just out to get the new guy wet. We should have bumper-locked Kenny and Patty all day and stuck even tighter to them at night, especially in a crowd like that. I know that. It will not happen again."

Mark started organizing the videos on his wall screen and turned to Billy. "I know that, man. You don't even need to say it. It happened. It won't again. Listen, Kenny walks all over the city all the time and never has problems. She comes into town and someone tries to kill him. You know how I feel about coincidences."

"I do. You don't believe in them. Anything else?"

"Yeah. Tell them to take down the videos out there. Eventually Kenny will get discharged, and I imagine that no matter what I say, he will at least stop by here to grab some things on his way home to rest. I don't want him seeing monster-sized images of himself getting his ass beat. I'll touch base with you soon."

. . .

Mark reviewed the videos in silence and brainstormed possible explanations.

Who is this guy and what's his problem? Billy is right. This was not completely random. But if he was specifically targeting Kenny and Patty, why would the attacker look so surprised—or pissed off—when he sees them across the street? Could he somehow know what Patty does for a living? Maybe's he's been on the receiving end of an offensive NSA cyber op and just happened to bump into her in an already angry crowd where she was a target of opportunity. Or was he a well-armed white supremacist who lost his mind when he saw a mixed-race couple? It looks like the bottle landed right in front of her, as if he was trying to hit her specifically.

Mark replayed, forward and backward half a dozen times, the part where the attacker threw the bottle. On his final viewing, he froze the frame, stood up, and approached the screen until his face was within inches of it.

"Hey. Somebody get in here."

A young analyst appeared at his door.

"See this guy right here? The guy in the white hat and the black turtleneck off to the side? You can't see his face very well because he has the turtleneck pulled up high and the hat pulled down low."

"Yeah. White hat. Black turtleneck. Got him."

"Watch his reaction when Kenny's attacker throws the bottle. Tell me I'm not crazy."

He played the video and waited for feedback.

"Honestly, just looks like some dude in a white hat to me. What do you see?"

"Look at it again. Watch him after the bottle gets thrown. He sees it clearly, because he's standing right behind the attacker and off to the left when he throws it. Other people naturally back away from him quickly, but not him. He just slowly creeps backwards until he disappears into the crowd, moving at a snail's pace compared to everyone else. And his eyes are scanning the scene the whole time as he fades away. Do you seriously not see that?"

"Yeah, I do, now that you mention it. That is weird. Want me to see what else I can find on him? If they were together, we should be able to find footage of them together somewhere close to that spot."

"Yes. Do that. And show me anything that seems the least bit anomalous."

Mark checked the time and gathered some of the things he would need to take to D.C. He would arrive home just in time to eat breakfast with Luci and the twins.

Mark cherished those precious few moments when he could put the security world on pause and immerse himself in their world. He would make silly jokes. The kids would laugh. Luci would smile and beam with pride about every little detail of their beautiful family.

Family. McDermott. Stay on top of her trip in real time. She should be almost there by now.

Mark checked the time. He shook his head and stopped his internal dialogue before it got started. *She'll be fine. She's not the first U.S. senator to take such a trip, and she won't be the last.* He pulled out his phone and sent her a quick text before watching the video of the attack one more time.

Okay, Luci. You wanted me to warm up just a little bit. Here it is.

MARK: Please be careful. Listen and follow all security protocols. I don't want news to break that you were there until you're long gone. Call when you return. I'll be in D.C. Be safe.

Mark returned his attention to the monitor.

"I've got my things and I'm going home to lie down for a while, Mark. Do you need anything before I go?"

The sound of Kenny's voice broke Mark's concentration. He paused the video and walked to the doorway.

"How are you feeling? Come in and sit down for a minute. I'm on my way out of town. How are you feeling? Any better?"

Mark waved through the door to David as Kenny took a seat on the sofa and leaned back.

"I've been better, but I was serious when I said it looks a lot worse than it is. Don't get me wrong—I feel like shit, but the concussion looks like it was relatively minor. We Harringtons have thick skulls, evidently."

Mark pointed to the screen. "Here's the attacker when he notices you two. The angle isn't great but you can see that he looks … I don't know … startled? Then he throws the bottle and starts screaming."

Kenny squinted to see the image more clearly, his vision still fuzzy from the earlier beating. "Yeah, that's him. Still no ID?"

"Not yet. Wish I knew what he was screaming, but we can't even try lip-reading from this angle."

"I just got a better one," said the returning young analyst as he entered Mark's office. "I wanted to get a better shot of the mystery guy in the white hat, and I just scored a video from a more street-level perspective. It's not helping much with the white hat, but you can get a much better look at the attacker." He tapped several controls on the monitor and the new video appeared.

"Much better. Not perfect, but a major improvement," Mark said, turning to Kenny. "We need to get this to Patty to see where and how she knows this guy. But I want you to get the rest you need. Go home and don't worry about any of this, okay? It's got nothing to do with you anymore. Your only mission is to get better."

Kenny was squinting and focusing on the video. He poured a sip of water into his dry, swollen mouth. "Help me out, Mark. Enlarge him, put him in the middle of the screen, and loop that part of the video for me, will you?"

Mark finished packing his things and put on his leather jacket. He watched the loop one more time. "I'm outta here. Let's shut this off and both go home, Kenny. You need rest, okay?"

Kenny did not answer. His one functioning eyelid was fluttering and he looked as if he had suddenly been choked purple. Mark dropped his bag and rushed to his side.

"Kenny? Kenny? You okay, brother? Can you hear me?"

Kenny began nodding his head deliberately and held up one finger, indicating that he needed a minute. Mark stood by anxiously as Kenny regained his breath and color.

"I'm okay … I'm okay."

"Good. What was all that about? Do we need to get you back to Mass General? Is it your ribs? Do they hurt like hell when you breathe too deeply?"

"Yeah." Kenny coughed lightly but grimaced as if stuck in the side with a hot poker. "But that's not it. Him … him," he said, pointing at the screen.

Mark looked over his shoulder at the looping video. "Him? What about him?"

"I know what he's yelling, Mark."

Mark snapped his head forward and looked at his beaten colleague. Kenny had regained his composure, but his purple face had turned a ghostly white. He looked terrified.

"Tell me." Mark stood up and approached the screen. "What's he saying? Looks to me like it's just one word he keeps repeating. What do you think it is?"

"I know what the word is, Mark. And I know who he is." Kenny stood up and joined Mark near the screen. "His name is Dmitri. He's Russian. I'm 100 percent certain."

Mark turned to face Kenny with a quizzical look.

"We'll get to how you know that in a minute. But first, tell me what the hell you think this Russian guy is yelling at Patty."

"He's not yelling at her. He's yelling at me, Mark."

"What's he yelling, Kenny?"

"He's yelling my name."

"Doesn't look like it."

"That's because he's not yelling 'Kenny.' He's yelling 'Hobbit,' over and over."

Mark looked confused and Kenny could see that he was losing patience. "Why Hobbit?"

"You really don't remember, Mark? He's yelling 'Hobbit' because that's who I was back then."

"Back when?"

"Back before you moved home and retired."

Kenny paused and expected his words to detonate in Mark's head.

Mark flashed back to the highlights of his final days in official government service, back when he proudly wore an American flag on his shoulder instead of the Imperium logo. Mark had returned home after a long absence to pay his respects to Agnes shortly after her death. While there, he had rekindled his on-again, off-again long-distance relationship with Luci. A terrorist attack pierced the town's Fourth of July celebration with violence. A brutish ATF agent named Frank Tagala helped Mark and Kenny identify the terrorist ring leader responsible. A rogue cop tried to kill Luci, and Mark disposed of him. Other than that, he was at a loss.

"What am I missing, Kenny?"

"Mark, don't you remember who identified that dirtbag Amir who shot up our town? I'll give you a hint. It's the same guy who jacked a drone and located Amir up in New Hampshire. He got locked up for it. Dunbar had to get him out. Remember him?"

"That was you, Kenny."

"No. It was the Hobbit. That was my hacker name back then."

CHAPTER THREE: The Promise

"Touchdown in five, Senator."

McDermott looked up at the crew chief and nodded. Then she nodded to the agent in charge of her Imperium security detail, a strong and confident woman named Sadie who appeared to be about thirty years old but who, if Mark's summary of her experience was accurate, would have been closer to forty. McDermott admired her warm smile and confidence. It made her feel safe, even where they were about to land. Sadie pointed to her own head covering to remind the senator to put hers on before touchdown.

The senator pulled the long scarf over her head and wrapped it tightly under her chin. Then she pulled out her phone and stared at the text message from Mark for a few more seconds. She squeezed the phone with both hands for several seconds, her eyes closed.

Maybe Luci is right. Maybe he cares more than he lets on. But for God's sake, Lois. You've had a forty-five-year pause in your relationship. He has a right to his own life. You can't reconnect and expect a fairytale ending, even though he did come to you. Consider yourself lucky just for knowing them. God, I'd give anything to just hug those adorable twins and tell them how lucky they are to have such special parents. Anything.

She unzipped the front pocket of her ski parka and stuffed her phone inside. Then she slipped on her gloves and chuckled at the last part of Mark's text.

Me, out of the news? Come on, Mark. I'm not even in the country and I'm still on the front page. Erosion of civil liberties. Gun control. Extremism. Stalled

Supreme Court Justice appointee James Midas. Pick a story and there's a good chance I'm mentioned in it somewhere.

McDermott's media coverage was something she had learned to live with. The haters weren't a surprise. Even Senator Johnson had warned her from the beginning: if you are going to pick a fight with the NRA or military-industrial complex, you'd better be ready for attacks. And she had been ready for them. What she hadn't been ready for was the backstabbing attacks from her own side.

What the hell is wrong with some of these people? Did they think I would ride into the U.S. Senate on a magical unicorn and miraculously change things overnight? That's not the way things work. It's a process, dammit.

Most people understood, but the vociferous sliver of her supporters who didn't moved leftward in search of their next savior. "Don't take it personally," the Democratic minority leader had said to her. "Voters are fickle. Just keep doing your thing and don't take it personally." Good advice. But sometimes things get too personal not to be taken personally.

Such was the case when Megan, McDermott's only other child and Mark Landry's half-sister, lost hope and moved on from McDermott's staff. But while the supporters who had abandoned McDermott went searching leftward, Megan went eastward, all the way to the Mediterranean, to find her own purpose.

Senator Lois McDermott had not seen her daughter in over a year—the longest they had ever been away from each other. This secret trip had taken more than a month to plan and coordinate. She looked at her watch.

Only three more minutes, Meg.

. . .

Sadie, the Imperium operator and agent in charge of security, tapped McDermott on the shoulder and pointed out the side window of the gray, unmarked Bell 412 helicopter. McDermott scooted closer to Sadie and peered out the window as the pilot brought the copter down onto a concrete pad the size of a postage stamp two thousand feet below. Then she directed her anxious gaze to the horizon.

The view of the refugee camp was awe-inspiring. People, tents, shacks, trucks, and shanties as far as the eye could see. Hundreds of thousands of people from across the war-torn Middle East and North Africa. A dim beehive of despair and uncertainty, all semi-contained by miles of barbed-wire fences and armed men.

"Remember, as soon as we touch down we're out and moving. One of my guys is already posted halfway between the helipad and the strong point where you'll meet with the camp administrator and staff. My guy is the line of demarcation. If anything happens between the bird and him, we return to the bird and emergency exfil immediately. If anything happens after we reach him, he will direct us to the nearest hard point."

McDermott nodded, smiled, and pretended not to be terrified.

When the Bell's skids hit the concrete, the side door swung open. Sadie and the senator exited first. Sadie was on the right, her left arm linked with the senator's right. Four Imperium operators immediately surrounded them in a diamond formation and they moved quickly toward the greeting party standing in front of the main administration tent.

The multinational leaders of the refugee camp extended their welcome and thanks to Senator McDermott for having the courage to visit and see the turmoil for herself.

"Senator, we have a few things planned for you during your very short time on the ground. But I also imagine that you'd like a few minutes to catch up with one of our most valuable leaders. I believe you know each other," said a tall, bulky Dutch lawyer and activist turned UN human rights official. "I will see you later."

He smiled and stepped to the side. Behind him, waiting patiently with an ear-to-ear smile and misty eyes, was Megan.

"Hi, Mom."

The two women hugged silently for several minutes with happy tears streaming down their faces. McDermott stepped back an arm's length and looked her daughter up and down. She thought Megan looked exhausted but knew better than to say anything.

"Okay, Mom. We've got limited time and they might decide to whisk you away at any second. So let's take a minute for you to freshen up. After that, we have a briefing prepared for you. Then I'm going to show you around a little bit. Sound like a plan?"

"Definitely. Anything you want."

...

The senator had several thoughtful questions for the staff but mostly sat quietly and listened during the briefing. The view from the helicopter had been overwhelming enough, but once she heard the numbers associated with the operation, she was astounded. More than three hundred thousand people, mostly Syrian, called the camp home.

Megan walked on the senator's left side holding onto her arm. Sadie walked on the senator's right and one or two steps in front, scanning continually as they walked slowly down a seemingly endless row of tents.

"I want to make sure we don't get too far from the aircraft, okay?" Sadie said into her lip microphone to the rest of the Imperium security detail, but also making sure to speak loudly enough for Megan to hear.

"It's right up here on the left," Megan answered, pointing in their direction of travel. "There's somebody really special I want you to meet, Mom."

Several aid workers held the door flap open. McDermott and Megan made their way past a row of patients to a curtained-off area at the far end of the tent.

"Her name is Asha. She wants to tell you her story if you'll listen."

Megan gently pulled back the curtain to reveal a Syrian woman in her early twenties. Her hands were clasped and resting on top of her swollen belly. McDermott figured that Asha must be well into her third trimester by now. A nurse was checking her blood pressure.

McDermott turned to her daughter. "Of course I'll listen."

...

Asha smiled warmly as they shared small talk through a simultaneous translator for several minutes. But the smile evaporated the moment she began sharing her story.

"She says life wasn't so bad for her and her family before the war started. They weren't rich but they were a lot better off than a lot of other people they knew, so they were always thankful for what they had," the translator explained, loudly enough for McDermott and Megan to hear but not so loudly as to drown out Asha's delicate voice.

The senator kept her eyes on the expecting mother and nodded understandingly to the translator.

"But things changed very quickly. The violence was nonstop, with suicide bombers, soldiers we had never seen before, Russian air strikes … all the killing, plus food, water, and medicine disappeared. Then the airstrikes finally forced everyone out of our side of the city."

McDermott struggled to maintain her composure as Asha recounted the horror she had gone through before coming to the refugee camp.

"She stayed as long as she could, even as family members were starting to disappear … either killed in the bombings or rounded up by the regime and never seen again. Finally, she and her husband scraped together everything they could and made their way to the Mediterranean, where they gave everything they had to a boat captain—a Syrian man everyone called Ahab."

Asha's contempt was palpable when she said his name.

Through the interpreter, she told of going to a small village on the Mediterranean coast along with what seemed like every other refugee fleeing the carnage. Which meant Ahab could easily raise his price per person. He did exactly that, unfazed by the pleas for mercy from the weary travelers. Ahab was well known for turning the final slot selections into games for the amusement of his crew, a lowly bunch just as sick as he. Mothers and fathers would be forced to appear before him and make their case as to why they should receive passage before others. He would laugh and make fun of their destitution, occasionally forcing fathers to fight each other, with the winner's family getting a secure spot on the boat.

When the Syrian refugees refused to fight for spectacle or survival, Ahab would scoff and think of other creative ways to differentiate the vulnerable population. For Asha and Tarik, that meant reaching deep down into the front pocket of his dirty trousers for a coin to flip.

Asha and Tarik won the toss, and Ahab promised that he would get them to the European mainland. She didn't know what happened to the other couple. Ahab promised to get them to European mainland. They thought they had it made at that point. She had no idea that the nightmare was just about to begin.

Megan looked at her watch. Then she quietly pulled the privacy curtain shut and motioned for Asha to continue. The senator's allotted time in the camp was almost up, and Megan wanted to make sure that she heard Asha's whole harrowing tale. The translator continued.

"Over four hundred people were crammed onto a ship that could safely transport maybe half that number. After a day in the open water, the ship's engine failed. They drifted for another day until an even smaller boat came out to meet them. When they were ordered to change ships, the crowd panicked and capsized the first boat. Hundreds of already starving people were now forced to swim to stay afloat. Many panicked and drowned immediately; some floated away; still others fought for the limited space on the new boat. Her husband, Tarik, tried to get them to the new boat but there was no use. It sailed away, leaving God knows how many people floating and clinging to each other. She and Tarik had a life preserver between the two of them. They were told that another boat would be coming. They drifted and floated for what seemed like an eternity. And then—"

The translator listened to Asha in silence. Then he turned to the senator and continued with the story. McDermott knew the next part would be painful.

"Tarik was very ill before they had even left home and had gotten weaker and weaker as he practically carried Asha all the way to the coast. After a day of floating and sharing one life preserver between them, he despaired and gave up. He kissed her, told her he loved her, and said that she and the baby would be better off with the life preserver to themselves ... and that any chances of a new life somewhere would be better without him. Then he let go and slowly drifted away forever. She floated for almost another entire day before being picked up by a fishing vessel and she eventually ended up here."

McDermott's eyes watered at the heartbreaking story and tears streamed down her face. She wiped them away. Then she squeezed Asha's hand and rested her other palm flat on her belly. The baby was moving.

"I'm so sorry, Asha. I am so sorry this happened to you."

The translator shared her words with the expectant mother, who managed a smile and a brief reply.

"She said she knows you are no stranger to loss."

McDermott reached over and held Megan's hand. Obviously, Megan had shared her own story with Asha. Megan's father, Jack, worked in the Twin Towers and was killed on September 11. Several years later, Megan's sister was gunned down in a school shooting in Connecticut. To say McDermott was no stranger to loss was an understatement.

"There's one more thing, Mom," Megan said.

Asha smiled broadly as tears flowed down both cheeks.

"At first, when Tarik mentioned her and the baby, she thought he was just losing his mind like many of the others. But when she finally reached the refugee camp and received a physical, it was confirmed," the translator continued.

"What was?" McDermott asked.

Megan answered, "The pregnancy. When Tarik gave up the life preserver for her and the baby, it was the first she had heard of it."

Asha pointed skyward. "Gawd."

Sadie opened the curtain, made eye contact with the senator, and held up her hand, indicating that they would be leaving the camp in five minutes. McDermott knew there would be no time for discussion.

She nodded at Sadie and leaned in closely to say goodbye to Asha. She stroked the young woman's hair.

"You are a beautiful, brave, and very special person. And that baby of yours will be lucky to have you. Thank you for letting me visit with you today."

McDermott and Megan were exiting the curtained-off area when Asha spoke again. She was asking a question. The translator looked the senator in the eyes and repeated the question.

"So what are you going to do about it?"

"Excuse me," answered McDermott.

"That's what she's asking. She wants to know how you're going to help."

McDermott looked back and forth between Asha and Megan several times. Megan was putting on her best poker face, but McDermott could read her daughter like a book. She was dying to hear the senator's answer to Asha's pointed question.

McDermott approached Asha's bedside again and placed a hand on her shoulder. The expression on the young woman's face was not unlike Megan's—earnest and intrepid, as if asking, "What are we waiting for?" And McDermott knew the similarities would not end there.

She would tell the suffering woman that it's complicated.

Asha would not understand why the people who could help were choosing not to do so.

McDermott would say again how complicated things are. She would say there are many moving parts and pieces to the puzzle. She would say this partially to make herself feel better about her own powerlessness. Asha would ask her to try as hard as she could. Then the senator would leave, knowing full well that the chances of real, measurable help for refugees were slim to none.

Megan had left the senator's staff and started working with refugees partially because she was sick and tired of being told how complicated things were in D.C. Gun control? No. Minimum wage increase? No. Education reform? Not this year. She was done with red tape. She wanted results. Now McDermott was being put on the spot and Megan fully expected to hear more empty promises.

"Asha. I know what you're thinking. You're wondering why people who could help are choosing not to. And I'm not here to make excuses for any of us. But I will promise you this: if there is anything I can ever do to help babies like yours"—she glanced in the direction of Asha's belly—"I will. And I don't care what it costs me politically. In fact, I am going to make it my priority. You can quote me. I promise you I am going to help. And I'll do something about Ahab as well. I promise."

Asha smiled when the translator finished and answered in broken English with a thumbs-up sign.

"Okay, thank you!"

...

The helicopter's rotors were moving and a member of McDermott's security detail was holding the aircraft door open, waiting for her to board.

"We need to be strapped in within the next two minutes, Senator. News has already broken that you are here. Some knucklehead didn't get the memo and tweeted about it right after we landed. We need to be in the air ASAP," said Sadie loudly, looking McDermott directly in the eyes.

"Thanks for coming. It was so good to see you, Mom. Even if you can't do anything to help, I really appreciate you coming and listening."

McDermott smiled and bowed her head. "I know what you must be thinking. More empty promises from a politician, right? Not this time, Meg. You've inspired me with your work here, and I have some catching up to do. I'll get right on it as soon as I get back to D.C. Promise. I love you."

"Love you too, Mom."

"Oh, and get me as much information as you can on this Captain Ahab guy. Statements from witnesses. Anything. Why do they call him Ahab? What's his real name? I want to see if I can get an international arrest warrant created."

"Will do."

The two women embraced until Sadie grasped McDermott by the right elbow and led her toward the waiting aircraft. McDermott and Megan kept their eyes on each other and waved back and forth as long as they could.

The helicopter lifted off, banked hard left, and ascended more quickly than any of McDermott's previous helicopter flights. Sadie put a hand on her shoulder to comfort her. The senator smiled and looked out over the horizon.

I won't let you down again, Megan. Even if it kills me, I will not let you down again.

. . .

"The man was a pig, Mark. An absolute pig of a human being."

"I get that. And I don't doubt you, Kenny. But I'm trying to process all this and I feel like I'm still missing something. Let me run through it one more time. You tell me if my summary is accurate so far."

"Okay, but I'm telling you he's the only person in the world who knows me. And it's because I burned him."

"I'll get to that. Let's back up and go through it again. Back in your freelance days—your Hobbit days or whatever—you did lots of different jobs for lots of different people. Some of them were unsavory. Got it. And I get the part about most hackers not just being willing to do anything for money. Some kind of geek code. Got that too. So you did some work for this guy's boss—what was his name again?"

"Boris. Boris the Jew is what everyone called him. Supposedly Serbian by birth but brought up in the Soviet Union by a man who amounted to a thief-in-law. Boris took the parts of the organized criminal code that suited his interests, tossed out the rest, and reacted brutally to anyone who tried to correct his ways. And like I said, the man was a pig. An absolute pig of a human being. If you knew the kinds of things he had his grubby paws into, it would shock even you, Mark.

He wasn't just some petty criminal, he was a demon. He trafficked in humans. He sold children. He murdered with impunity. And although he was a pig, he was way ahead of the curve in leveraging technology to his advantage.

"When I found out just how bad he was, I decided immediately to sabotage him. I set him up. Slowly transferred things around and in one fell swoop emptied one of his main accounts from a small private bank in western Russia. I saw an opportunity to redistribute some ill-gotten wealth and I did it. That was it. It really wasn't that big of a deal."

"How much was it?"

Kenny finished his water and threw the empty plastic bottle in the recycle bin. "I don't really remember. But I guess it was a lot."

"Don't do this, Kenny. Don't make me pull teeth. How much was it?"

Kenny looked upward at the ceiling and nodded his head back and forth as if counting. "In total—I don't know, like maybe six or seven. No more than seven."

"Kenny," said Mark in a firm voice. Kenny was startled and snapped his attention back to Mark. "Seven what? Tell me right now."

"Seven million."

"Seven million dollars? Are you telling me you once boosted seven million dollars from Russian criminals and this is the first I'm hearing of it?"

"Euros, actually. And yes."

"Wait here." Mark opened his office door and grabbed the first analyst who was walking by. "Come here. I want you to take care of this right now." They walked to the nearest table and Mark put down the two photographs. Put out an INTERPOL Black on the dead guy and make sure everyone here knows not to share his identity with anyone. I want to see who, if anybody, shows up with information. Also, put out an INTERPOL Blue on the guy in the white hat, as well as a New England–wide BOLO. If anyone gets anything on his identity or current whereabouts, I want to know immediately. Thank you. You can go."

Sending the analyst on his way with a slap on the back, Mark returned to his office and shut the door.

"Okay, Kenny. So what happened then? You got away with the money and nobody ever came looking for you?"

"It would have been almost impossible. None of them know my real identity. Besides, I didn't take the money for myself, Mark. I gave almost all of it away. Charities, causes. Yeah, I admit I did buy myself a few things, but most of that money was quickly given out. Gone. So there was nothing for them to recover. Besides, Boris the Jew got killed just a few weeks later. Tortured and beaten, old-school Soviet style. And he deserved it."

"I'm sure he did. And I'm sure losing seven million dollars didn't help."

"Euros, actually."

Mark made Kenny wait as he scrolled through an email on his desktop and confirmed an encrypted message on his phone.

SADIE: Package is safe. Feet dry in Milan. Awaiting refueling, then home to D.C. All is well.
MARK: Roger. Keep me informed.

"Listen, Kenny, I'm not going to bother sending you home to rest because I know you'll be a pain in the ass about it. I also think you're safer here than anywhere else until we get a handle on things. I need to get to D.C. Keep me informed on everything and have the VR footage of last night's Billings, Montana raid sent to the plane. I know there were several casualties that Dunbar is bound to ask about. I want to see the POV footage myself before I land so I know what I'm talking about."

"Will do. And listen, I'm sorry, Mark. I never thought there was a snowball's chance in hell I'd see that guy again. This is my fault. I'll do whatever I can to help fix it. I'm with you, man. You have my loyalty. I want you to know that. It's important for me to know that you know that."

Mark looked into Kenny's exhausted eyes and nodded. "I know that, Kenny. I've never doubted that. So let's stay on top of things, okay?" Mark started to exit and shouted back over his shoulder. "Somebody make sure I have all McDermott's vital info, and I want her location sent to me in real time, starting right now until she lands in D.C. That is all for now. Goodbye."

Mark walked past the elevator and opted for the stairs instead, reflecting on Kenny's shocking revelation as he shuffled downward. He was not happy about his paucity of specific knowledge regarding Kenny's past, but of course there were plenty of things from Mark and the Family's past that Kenny was not privy to.

You are full of surprises, Kenny Harrington. But it's hard to get too mad at you. And this happened, after all, because you stuck it to a brutal predator who trafficked in children among other things. And now you're on my side. One of my guys.

He turned the final corner and walked through the open door into the private Imperium underground garage. He pushed a button and his Range Rover's engine sprang to life as he climbed inside.

I always knew there was more to you, Kenny. Call it intuition. And I guess I was right. But I've felt the same way toward McDermott on more than one occasion as well. Like she's always holding something back—or even outright hiding something from me. Maybe I'm making too much of it.

...

When the Imperium-owned Gulfstream G280 reached its cruising altitude for the short flight to D.C., Mark pulled his VR goggles from his travel bag and strapped them to his head. It took him several seconds to adjust to the HD POV footage of a nighttime raid on suspected anti-government extremists plotting an attack in Montana. He had already read the full report submitted by Max, the team leader, but since a fatality had occurred, he wanted to see firsthand how things had unfolded.

Three far-right extremists had gone from being on the watch list to twenty-four-hour surveillance to imminent threat in less than two weeks' time. The word *militia* was used several times in the report, but the extremists had no affiliation with known organizations. These three were rejects who had been tossed out of every militia meeting they attended, because nobody was buying what they were selling or because others suspected that the mouthy misfits were government plants sent to entrap them.

The three had planned on driving from Montana to Seattle, Washington, where they would blow up a large mosque with a vehicle-borne improvised explosive device (VBIED). On their way home the next day, they intended to assassinate an abortion provider and several of his nurses. They were delusional, but delusional men can cause catastrophic damage, as Timothy McVeigh showed America in 1995. Images of the Oklahoma City bombing that turned the Alfred P. Murrah Building into an open-faced doll house flashed in Mark's mind. McVeigh's name would be tied around the militia movement's neck like a noose from that moment forward.

Mark cued the video and adjusted the volume so that he could see and hear the operation from Max's point of view. His line of sight through the open door of the house was unobstructed. The camera momentarily went dark as the operators waited for the flashbang to detonate inside. They burst into the home a split second afterwards.

Since the Imperium team had been sworn and temporarily deputized by state authorities—a process known as sheep dipping—the surveillance and raid were perfectly legal. But Mark needed to check off the legal and procedural boxes as he watched the video unfold.

The operators' voices came through loud and clear as they overwhelmed the two would-be terrorists on the sofa and loveseat. The third had taken off down a narrow hallway on Max's side of the room. Max gave the man clear commands to stop and get down on the floor. Instead, the man kept running and darted into a room at the far end of the hall. Max, an experienced former Special Forces Operational Detachment-Delta (SFOD-D) operator, followed closely with good reason to believe that he would have to shoot the suspect.

Nonlethal entry. Check. First bad guy to move is usually going to be a problem. Check. Where is he going? To get a weapon? Kill a hostage? Push the doomsday button? Dunno. So you gotta stick on him like white on rice.

When Max neared the open bedroom door, he slowed his pace and eased his way slowly around the corner, "slicing the pie" with the muzzle of his suppressed M4. He completed only two pieces of the pie before the suspect emerged from a closet with a Springfield M1A in his hands. The weapon was clearly visible thanks to Max's green tactical light.

Means. Check. Intent. Check.

Two quick trigger presses and the suspect dropped to the floor. The team cleared the rest of the home without incident. The video ended as they began the intelligence collection phase of the operation.

Mark removed his VR goggles and wrote a few notes on his laptop about the operation. There is no such thing as a textbook example raid in the real world, but this one had been close. The team had done their homework, planned, rehearsed, and executed an operation that likely saved lives but that nobody would ever hear about.

Seeing the video made Mark proud. And it also reminded him of how badly he wanted to get out into the field. He had valued his player-manager role at Imperium and promised himself that he would always keep a foot in the field, like Dunbar in his younger days. But he had been bogged down in the office recently, and the video lit a fire inside.

God damn. I gotta get out into the field soon.

Mark removed the VR goggles and returned them to his travel bag. Then he stood up, stretched a bit, and walked the length of the aircraft's main cabin several times before reclining back in his seat and initiating a video chat with Kenny.

"Anything new on White Hat?"

"Nothing yet, but I know we're pulling out all the stops. Hopefully we'll get a break somewhere, but it could take a while."

"Question, Kenny. The dead guy. Why throw a bottle then sucker punch you? If he wanted you dead, why not just shoot you in the head?"

"No idea. Can't answer for him. But I do remember he liked to stay drunk. He was a true dirtbag, Mark. A street thug."

"How did he know what you look like?"

"Who?"

"Dmitri, the dead guy. You said he was the only person who ever connected your face with the Hobbit moniker. How did that happen? You either left that part out or we never got to it before I left the office. How did he know what you looked like?"

There was a long pause as Kenny pretended to be reading his screen. Then he looked back into the camera. "Because he saw me at the bank making the final financial transactions."

"What bank? Where? You mean you didn't do all of this virtually? You actually walked into a bank and walked out with seven million dollars, no, euros?

"I wanted to do it all virtually but I couldn't, so I had to Shawshank them."

"Shawshank?" Mark thought for a second. "What does that mean? You crawled through a tunnel of shit or something? Start making sense, Kenny."

"I created a credible false identity, got fake credentials confirming that identity, then waltzed into the local bank dressed to the nines and withdrew or transferred it all. But the bank wasn't local. That would be almost impossible."

"Now you have me pulling teeth again, Kenny. Where the hell was the bank?"

"I already told you, it was in western Russia."

Mark sat up in his chair. "You traveled to western Russia to steal the money?"

"Yes. But it's not like I went to Moscow or something. I went to Norway on a vacation package and passed into Russia on its westernmost border. I was in and out of the country in hours."

"You're a big boy. You're entitled to your privacy. But I really wish I would have known some of this before, Kenny. Now tell me, what role did the dead guy play in this international money-laundering operation of yours? And please just cut to the chase."

"I arranged for him to pick me up at the Norwegian border and give me a ride."

Mark stood up paced the cabin floor. He waved through the open cockpit, letting the crew know that he was aware they were about to descend into Washington, D.C.

"I'm surprised he didn't get whacked back then. Or maybe before anyone could find out how badly he had been played, he turned on and helped knock off Boris. Regardless, it easily explains why he wanted you dead. You stole seven million euros on his watch, and to add insult to injury, you tricked him into driving the getaway car. Jesus, Kenny. And you deemed this too minor to bring up when Dunbar put you on the team?"

"Excuse me. It's not like I ever really had a job interview, Mark. And you aren't very chatty about a lot of your past either. I'm sorry about this, but there's nothing I can do about it now."

The Gulfstream began to descend toward Reagan Washington National Airport. Mark fastened his seatbelt in preparation for landing.

"I know that. Let's keep moving forward. But do me a favor and stay out of the field. You are one hell of a cyber-operator and developing nicely as an analyst, but this is why you are not a field operator. Loose ends, my friend, are never good and this is why. Understand?"

Kenny was contrite but seemed annoyed at the reminder to stay out of the field, as if he had been planning to storm the Bastille alone or something. "Yeah, I understand. And you've made it quite clear in the past where my place is. Look, I've told you everything I know about this guy. I can talk about the cyber ops I did to pull it all off, but trust me, your ears will start to spill blood after the first few hours. You're the boss. You tell—"

Mark cut him off. "Okay, good. We're on the same sheet of music. I'll talk to you later, okay? I'm about to touch down and have a few things to do."

He turned off the monitor and looked out the window at the D.C. skyline during the final thirty seconds of descent. He thought about his upcoming dinner with Dunbar and wondered what the old man wanted to talk about so badly. Maybe he had decided on an official timeline for his retirement. Probably sometime in the next two or three years, if Mark had to guess. Or maybe he just wanted to talk about the old days. Either way, Mark Landry had an intuitive feeling that opportunity was about to knock. And he was more than ready to answer.

What was Kenny going on about? Something about the technical explanation behind his one-man Russian operation ... that it would make me bleed out my ears. That's probably true. Too much detail ... wait a minute. Bleeding. Blood. That's it. That's what I needed to doublecheck.

Mark fired up his laptop, located his files relating to Senator Lois McDermott's security detail, and opened the secure folder. Then he opened the senator's personal data information and medical history and whistled as he reviewed it. His phone vibrated in his pocket. A text from Dunbar.

DUNBAR: Move up meeting by an hour ... will explain later.
MARK: Roger.

Everyone is just full of surprises lately. I wonder what yours will be, Dunbar. Whatever it is, I'm ready to listen. Trusting you has never served me wrong.

CHAPTER FOUR: The Meeting

Dunbar greeted Mark with a warm hug when he arrived at the small, out-of-the-way family eatery located less than an hour northwest of Washington. The dining room crowd was sparse and quiet as Mark followed behind his normally spry mentor, wondering what in the hell had happened to him over the past few months. Dunbar didn't look much different, but he was noticeably slower, as if age was finally starting to catch up and he was losing his step. Mark's theory was validated when the hostess invited them to choose their own table and Dunbar opted for one closest to the men's room. That was something he never would have done before.

"They'll bring our food out in a little while. I hope you don't mind, but I ordered in advance because I have some pressing things to do later. And so do you," remarked Dunbar as he settled into his seat. Their server placed a bottle of Johnnie Walker Black between them and Dunbar smiled warmly.

"My doctor told me I should give this stuff up. I told him some things are worth dying for."

Dunbar and Mark raised glasses and looked into each other's eyes. Dunbar's looked like two pools of tears on the verge of spilling over. Noticing where he was focused, he winked at Mark, just to demonstrate that he could still read the younger man's mind.

"I feel a lot better than I look, Mark. I'm getting older but I'm far from dead."

They enjoyed friendly conversation through the meal, but without getting into any current business.

"Stop me if I've told you this before, Mark. I might have."

Mark nodded. Then he took the final bite of his cider-glazed pork chop and washed it down with a sip of wine. "I haven't." He was lying.

"Just a few days after starting in the business, I found myself in the middle of the Ia Drang Valley. And since we had a single-engine Piper Cub at our disposal, my boss at the time decided to give me some flying lessons. So he takes me up for maybe two or three touch-and-goes to show me how it's done."

Mark knew what was coming but pretended to be surprised.

"Then he tells me to make the next one a full stop. Which I did. And I about died when he popped the door and hopped out. 'Go ahead, kid. Let me see you do a few on your own.' Can you imagine? After about thirty minutes of flight training. Sounds crazy. But that was the way things were done back then. My mentors were old-school men. Lord, they don't make them like that anymore."

Mark smiled and leaned forward. "That's not necessarily a bad thing, though, is it? Remind me never to fly with you again."

"Hell, maybe you're right. But it all worked back then. For those times. But I guess things change. So we all have to change too. Or get out of the way, right?"

Dunbar's last comment sounded more declarative than reflective. Mark's radar was pinged. Dunbar was getting to the purpose of the meeting. The older man drained his glass and then leaned back in his chair.

"You remember how we met, right? Of course you do. Everyone remembers how they first got tapped, chosen, invited to join—whatever they call it these days." The Johnnie Walker Black and wine had made Dunbar more relaxed than Mark had seen in years.

"I do. I do. Somewhere out in the sandbox in Iraq. Mess hall. You sat down and changed my life." Mark finished his drink and leaned both forearms on the edge of the table.

"No, you changed your own, Mark. I offered you something. I gave you an option. But *you* made the choice that inevitably changed your life. Not me."

He said it with a smile. Mark couldn't tell if he was simply clarifying the record or subtly distancing himself from the decision. He sat silently and waited for Dunbar to continue.

"You were like me as a young soldier, at a crossroads in your career. Always looking for a mountain to climb. Wondering to yourself if there was anything bigger and better out there. You were ready too, weren't you?"

"I was. No doubt."

"The Ranger Regiment took good care of you, Mark. Prepared you well—there's no doubt about that. You're one of the best operators I've ever worked with, and that's coming from a career that's spanned several centuries."

Dunbar laughed awkwardly. Mark knew something was coming and tried to be patient.

Wait for it. Wait for it.

"It's time, Mark."

There it is.

"Time for what?"

"Time for me to retire. I'm far from being put out to pasture, but I'm close enough to know it's time to bow out gracefully. I've got a few things on my bucket list I've been wanting to do and it's time to do them. It's time for me to officially turn over command of Imperium to you. Assuming you're interested."

Dunbar already knew Mark was interested. They had been discussing this for several years, and Dunbar had taken Mark under his wing and introduced him to most of the people in his rolodex. He had been running the day-to-day operations for almost two years. Mark wondered why he was asking again. There must be more.

"I am. And I'm honored. You know that. What else is going on, Dunbar?" asked Mark as he leaned back, wiped his mouth with his napkin, and quickly scanned the room.

Black suit. Blue shirt. Red tie. Short brown hair. Clean-shaven. Sitting alone at a small table at the back of the room. Why are you paying so much attention to us, buddy?

Mark returned his attention to Dunbar, whose eyes had gone misty. "I will support you 100 percent, whatever decision you make."

Mark nodded slowly in acknowledgment. He felt his adrenaline surge and was transported back more than a decade to a small forward operating base in Iraq where he first met Dunbar. He smiled at his mentor. "I'm listening."

"Okay, here it is. Some serious changes are about to take place in D.C. Upper-level cabinet changes. Some pretty serious inside baseball I can't discuss, but I'm sure you understand that. The bottom line is this, though: you'll be taking over Imperium, so the future of the company is up to you. If you want to keep things the way they are—no problem, that's your decision. You're the commander. However, if you're willing to serve—and if you think the rest of the team is too—then you may have another option."

"Okay. What option is that?"

Dunbar reached across the table and placed his hand on Mark's forearm. "You see the man in the black suit standing at the back of the room?"

Mark looked around to find that the man he had spotted earlier was now standing next to a door in the back corner.

"Go to him. He'll take you to Senator Johnson, who is dining alone in the private room. He's expecting you."

Dunbar read Mark's expression and preempted his question. "Yes, Senate Majority Leader Johnson. But he's also a close personal friend of the President, and there's going to be some cabinet shuffling soon. He'll be resigning his seat to become national security advisor. The party won't lose the seat. The North Carolina governor gets to appoint someone to serve until a special election can be held. The Dems don't have anyone on the bench so it'll stay in the party. He's doing this because the President begged him, and he has received assurance that he'll be able to run things on his own terms. The president has been pushing for reconstitution of the Family, reporting directly to Johnson once he's national security advisor. Unfortunately, Johnson's not sold on the idea. He sees it as just another entity to manage. The president knows the value, but will defer to Johnson on the final decision. You need to impress Johnson. This is it, Mark. This is what we've been waiting for. No more of this private military contractor crap."

Mark took a long slow sip of his water and breathed deeply.

My chance. At last.

"You've met Johnson before, helped me brief him once or twice. You should know he's considering a few other outfits besides Imperium."

Mark felt his pulse quicken and took another sip of his water.

"Other outfits? There are no other outfits. Sure, there are some good guys out there doing good work, but nobody anywhere near what my team can do. Not even close. And they all know it."

Dunbar smiled widely. "You're telling the wrong guy, Mark. Go tell Johnson. If that's what you want. Just keep in mind that door-kickers are a dime-a-dozen in his view. If you want to impress him, you'll need to offer something nobody else can."

Mark reached across the table and put his hands on top of Dunbar's. His skin felt cold and paper-thin. When he started to speak, Dunbar cut him off.

"It's time, Mark. We'll catch up later. For now, I'm hopping out of the plane. It's time for you to fly solo."

Mark nodded and rose to his feet. He buttoned his suit coat and checked the time out of habit.

Showtime, Landry. Let's do this.

The twenty paces to the back of the room happened in slow motion as Mark reflected on what the first forty-five years of his extraordinary life had given him. He had a beautiful wife and children at home who loved and needed him. As a private military contractor, he had made more money than he could have ever dreamed of. Twenty years of active duty special-operations experience had prepared him for just about any tactical scenario that life could throw at him.

And yet the greatest pearl of wisdom he took with him was something Agnes had ingrained into him as a young man, one of what she called the keys to success.

"Stand up straight, Mark. Be confident. And when you walk into a room, act like you belong there."

The man in the black suit stretched out his hand as Mark arrived at the back table. "Are you Master Sergeant Landry?"

Mark gripped the other man's hand firmly and looked him squarely in the eyes.

"I used to be. Now it's just Mark. Mark Landry."

. . .

"Satellites don't just magically collide with each other for no reason. The Chinese can play dumb all they want, but we know better. They hacked into the navigation systems of those satellites. Now we have cyber war in outer space to worry about. So add that to the list."

Mark nodded and pretended to sip from the glass of Jack Daniels he had declined but was served anyway. Senator Johnson did not like to drink alone and it was obvious he had already had a few glasses. For more than thirty minutes, Senator Johnson had bounced from topic to topic with no logical or common thread tying it all together. He had yet to ask Mark a single substantive question.

Where the hell is he going with all this? Is he pulling a "drunken Ivan"? Russian diplomats and KGB types used to pull that one. They would act drunk so people wouldn't take them seriously and would drop their guard. Or maybe he's just unwinding. God knows how many irons he must have in the fire at any given time. Keep listening. Jump in at the right time.

"When the first non-state actor acquires a WMD, that's when the shit really hits the fan. That's when everything will change. But what if it's a digital WMD, hmm? Some sort of cyber nuke? How will that change the equation?" He took a long sniff of his glass, followed by a small sip. "It's tough to know who's got what these days. It ain't like the old days when the bad guys were nice enough to have parades and drive their latest weaponry up and down the street. No, nuh-uh. The only way to show off your cyber assets is to use them. The only happy people are the game theorists who can't remember the last time policymakers paid any attention to them."

Mark nodded and observed Johnson closely. The senator's tie was loosened and the top two buttons on his dress shirt were undone. Other than that, he was as impeccable as usual. A regal man with a presence. And evidently a buzz.

"Dunbar earned most of his stripes during the Cold War. Espionage, operating covertly within authoritarian regimes—that's his bread and butter. And he was one of the best, no doubt. But I support his decision to retire. He's not the right guy at the right time anymore. Not this time. But he tells me you are." Johnson put down his bourbon and took a long sip of ice water. "Well, I need someone close to me who can do more than shoot and scoot or collect dots. Collecting dots is easy; connecting them is a whole different ballgame. I need someone who can think big, understand strategic visions, grasp the future. Someone with multiple tools in their toolkit. Someone willing to do whatever it takes for our national security. Like Pompey the Great did for the Romans. Pirates were running amok in the eastern Mediterranean, messing up Roman trade something fierce. Pompey mopped them up and did his part to keep the republic around a little bit longer. I know you've been tested. I know you've faced those decisions and did what you had to do."

Mark knew he was referring to the Berlin mission. Johnson didn't have to come right out and say it. Still, Mark wondered how much of the story he actually knew. Very few people knew the entire story. Mark redirected the conversation.

"Senator. I understand your need for all of those things. But Pompeius Magnus had a blank check and free rein to do what he needed to do. I don't expect that. But can I assume that the new unit will be able to operate independently of the PMC Wall?"

Johnson looked as if he had been expecting the question. The Private Military Contractor Wall—a collection of statutes limiting access to information and resources without specific authorization—was a thorn in Mark's side at Imperium. He and the rest of the team dealt with it by bending the rules as far as they could and occasionally throwing them out the window, but they could only get away with so much. Considering the majority of leakers and whistleblowers over the past decade turned out to be private contractors – the oversight was reasonable. But Mark wanted to return to the old days when the Family could get AC-130 Spectre gunship or MC-12W Liberty support with minimal notice or oversight. He feared that those days might be gone forever. And the thought of spending the rest of his life in private security – separated by a wall not just from critical mission information, but from the nobility and honor of official government service.

"Dunbar says I should consider myself lucky to have you. Or something like that."

Mark smiled and sipped his bourbon. "That sounds like him, Senator. He's one of those old-school bosses who would go to hell and back for his people. He speaks like a proud father. Try not to hold it against me."

"No worries, son. And I understand why he's deciding to slow things down a bit. Hell, if I didn't have the crack staff I do to keep me up to speed on things, I would have long ago outlived my usefulness. Dunbar's a wise man. And rare is the man who passes on the opportunity for power. That's when you really find out what somebody is made of. It's easy for folks to say they don't care about power or money when they have neither. Introduce an opportunity to gain either one, and folks will seek power and money with a desire that—"

Mark finished the quotation: " 'A desire that ceaseth only in death.' And I agree. Hobbes was right."

Senator Johnson raised his glass in salute and finished his bourbon. "Exactly. Good. You're a well-read man. A rarity these days. Where'd you study? West Point?"

Mark smiled and shook his head. "Academy? No, Senator. I started my studies in the basement of a church with a Catholic priest. He taught me most of what I know. After high school, I went straight to Fort Benning. Infantry. Then Ranger school and into the 75th Ranger Regiment. I was there for twelve years. Then one day Dunbar recruited me and I was with him for a little over eight years."

"Family?"

"Married. Twin five-year-olds. No other family."

Mark thought to himself what Johnson's face would like if he continued with "Oh, and by the way, Senator Lois McDermott is my mother, but nobody knows that except my wife and a hacker called the Hobbit."

"Hmmm." The senator was soaking it all in, but he also appeared to be tiring. "Well, Mr. Landry, I appreciate your time this evening and I enjoyed our little chat. I trust that you'll keep me informed on anything significant—especially if you get any new information about your Russian incident in Boston. Those sneaky bastards have a way of creating problems where none exist and then exacerbating the situation. Our intel folks do a good job domestically, but they're also stretched pretty thin and can't track them all. If you discover anything, be sure to let us all know. We need all hands on deck."

"Will do."

Johnson waved for the restaurant manager to bring the bill. Mark checked his watch. He felt good about the meeting. He felt confident that he had impressed Johnson with his intellect and temperament. But if he was reading Johnson accurately, the senator had little interest in reestablishing the Family again—Mark could see it in his eyes. It was like a punch in the gut. Everything he'd hoped for disappearing on one man's whim.

"Did you have everything you needed tonight, Senator? Is there anything else we can do for you? Dessert is on the house if you are interested."

Johnson added a generous tip and signed the check. "I think you've done all you can for me, Vincent. That is, unless you have a few tricks up your sleeve that'll help pass the new budget and get J. J. Midas confirmed."

The manager shook Johnson's hand. "I wish I did. But you're the only one with that kind of power. You could always invoke the nuclear option and get things done with 51 votes. But I'm sure you're sick of hearing that, so I'll concentrate on doing my job and let you do yours. Thank you for coming, Senator. You are always welcome here."

After he left, Johnson looked back at Mark. "He's a good man," he said of the waiter.

"Have you ruled out changing the rules? It's all just based on a handshake agreement with the Democratic leader, right? I'm curious. Sorry if I'm out of line."

Johnson stood and started to slowly put on his winter coat. "Normally, I would say yes. But the bourbon has warmed me up a bit. The real answer is no. It's not because of a handshake agreement. It's because of my wife."

"Your wife, Sir?" Mark followed the senator toward the rear exit.

"Exactly. My wife has never had a cross word with anyone throughout my political career and is well-known for her gregarious nature. Once she mentioned to the opposition leader if he ever really wanted my word on something, a handshake might not do it but asking me for my promise as a Southern gentleman would. Well, that's what he did. And I promised. So, it's a combination of U.S. Senate tradition, which I hold dear, and Southern pride, which I hold sacred. As for my wife, I no longer leave her unattended in the presence of Democrats."

"I respect that. You are a man of your word."

"A Southern man of my word, Mr. Landry. I've still managed to get most of the party's agenda through this session, but I haven't had much luck with filling SCOTUS."

Mark could sense that the SCOTUS nomination was keeping Johnson up at night. "Then I'll be sure to not just keep you posted on the Russian investigation," he replied. "If I think of a way to secure the sixtieth vote for Judge Midas, I'll be sure to call as well."

"Please do, Mr. Landry." Johnson laughed dismissively at the comment, zipped up his thick coat, and stuffed his hands into the deep lambskin lined pockets. "Please do."

Mark stood and watched Senator Johnson exit the building. Then he reentered the main dining room and nodded to the staff on his way out the front door.

Johnson thinks I'm kidding. But Dunbar is probably right. Door kickers are a dime a dozen in Johnson's world, so he doesn't particularly respect or care about those who do that part of the job. If I want this, I have to offer something nobody else can deliver.

Mark imagined that any competing organization qualified enough to be considered for the job would likely be highlighting its tactical capabilities. Direct action raids. Deep surveillance. Hostage rescue. Snatch missions. Executive protection. Targeted assassination. Disruption.

But can they deliver the sixtieth confirmation vote for a Supreme Court nominee? Because I think I can.

CHAPTER FIVE: Decisions, Decisions

"I want another baby!" Luci screamed.

Mark stopped punching the heavy bag and turned around to find her standing at the bottom of the basement stairs. He had been at it for a while, and sweat was pouring down his body. He put his hands on top of his head and breathed deeply. "What did you say?"

"I said I want another baby."

"No you don't. You're joking, right?"

"Not really. Kind of. Okay, yes. But I've been standing here talking to you for two minutes and you haven't so much as acknowledged my existence."

Mark looked her up and down. She was wearing a white T-shirt that came to just above her navel and black panties with a pink bow on the front. Her long black hair was still wet from the shower. She sat on the bottom step holding a bottle of moisturizer between her knees as she dried her hair with a towel.

"Sorry, babe. I'm just distracted. What was the question again?"

Two calls you need to return. First, Andy called and says you owe him big time."

"Why?"

"Because it cost him a chunk of the town's budget to pacify the custodians union. All thanks to your active shooter training last week."

Mark smiled and thought of his close friend, the town's mayor, getting berated by school officials. When the police department had asked Mark to help train officers how to respond to an active shooter at the local high school, he had initially declined. But when Luci said that not helping would make both of them look bad and reminded him that their two children were in the local school system, he reconsidered— with the caveat that the training would have to be realistic or it would be a waste of time. When officers responded to the drill and entered the school, the fire alarm and sprinklers were already going off, drenching the classrooms in water. Role players of all ages were covered in blood. Mark was not surprised that quite a bit of overtime was needed to clean up.

"Andy will get over it. And so will the custodians union when they get their overtime checks. That was a good day of training. The cops loved it. Who else called?"

"Doc. He says he's been waiting for a callback for a week."

"Did he sound mad?"

"No, he's been busy. She didn't respond to the latest round of treatment. She's not doing well."

Mark pictured Doc sitting at his wife's bedside, changing IVs, giving medication, and telling her over and over how much he loved her. And how sorry he was that he had spent the majority of their marriage deployed. She had already been diagnosed by the time he retired. Now it sounded as if it was just a matter of time.

"I don't want to bother him. Not when he has much bigger things to worry about than me."

"He said you would say that and told me to remind you how important it is to talk to someone. It's normal, Mark. Everyone has things they need to talk about."

No shit, Luci. But I'm not like everyone. So I can't just talk to anyone. I've told you that.

Mark felt guilty. It wasn't as if he were blowing off some run-of-the-mill shrink. Doc had been Mark's direct boss and mentor when they had both worked for Dunbar in The Family. As a consequence, any details of Mark's career Doc didn't already know by heart were available to him one way or another. So it was reasonable that he would have concerns about the latent psychological impact of Mark's experiences.

"Got it. I'll call him."

He removed the soaked gray T-shirt and latched gravity boots around the ankles of his bare feet. Then he reached up, grabbing with both hands the chin-up bar drilled into the unfinished rafters and bringing his feet to the bar in one smooth motion. He hooked the boots around the bar and hung freely, upside down. Murphy wandered over from his dog bed and started licking his master's face. Mark dug his hands into the fur behind the dog's ears and scratched. "Kisses for daddy, Murphy. That's a good boy, yes. You love me, don't you? You look sad. What's wrong, boy? Are you dying to get back into the field too? Don't worry. Soon."

"So what are you going to do about the thing with Johnson? Even just from what you felt you could tell me, it sounds huge if it comes through. Are you going to take it if he offers it to you?"

"You already know what I think. It's once-in-a-lifetime chance that very few people ever get. But right now I don't have a warm and fuzzy feeling. I need to impress him but have no idea how."

He didn't tell her that he planned on throwing everything he had at influencing Senator McDermott to vote for Judge James Midas's confirmation. He just didn't know how yet.

Tell me, what do you think?"

"I know you get bored sometimes and want to do more. It's in your blood. But you still sacrificed career opportunities so you could be a father to your kids. Hell, during the first two years of their lives they spent more time with you than me. You'll always be there when we need you—we know that. And since you'll be in command you won't be doing a lot of door-kicking yourself, right?"

"Yeah, sure."

"No, I need more than a 'yeah, sure' on that, Mark. Things are different now. You're a father. We need you. So promise me you won't be taking any unnecessary risks."

"Promise."

"Then I think you should do what makes you happy. And know that I support whichever decision you make. You're a great father and husband. That'll never change. So if you think you have a chance to play at that level, go for it. What does Billy say?"

Mark bent at the waist and used his abdominal muscles to lift his hands up to the bar. He rested there for several seconds before letting go and slowly lowering himself back into a full hang. The relief on his spine felt euphoric. "He doesn't know. Neither does Kenny. I can't really talk to them about it because it's different. It's hard to explain."

"No, it's not. You're the boss for a reason. Billy and Kenny are both great—I love them. But you're the ringleader. You always have been."

"I've always been a good operator and leader, but honestly, I never thought I'd be in this position. Never in a million years. But what about you, Big Shot? How many different offers do you have so far?"

"Three," she answered with a smile. "Got the third today."

"What is it? Fill me in," said Mark as he folded his arms and started to do lunges.

"The Governor offered me a position at MEMA."

"Did he speak to you about it personally?"

"Nope. Staff."

Mark grasped the bar with both hands, unhooked his feet, and slowly lowered them to the concrete basement floor. "Say no."

"Why?"

"Because you shouldn't be some midlevel director somewhere. Neither of us should. It's time to go big or go home. So say no. If he wants you that badly, he'll come at you with a better offer. Trust me, once you accept a position, it's too late to negotiate, so ask for the world now while you can."

Luci was rubbing moisturizer on her legs. She paused and looked up. "So I should say no because they won't make me the boss on day one? That makes perfect sense."

"Thank you. I thought so. I've been thinking about it a lot the past few weeks. And I'm sure the perfect position will come along for you. I can feel it."

"Maybe I won't do anything. I'll just retire. Sit around and eat. Maybe work the occasional traffic detail or forty-fives tournament at the Knights of Columbus."

"No way. You'd lose your mind."

Mark toweled off and approached the stairs, where he got down on his knees. He squeezed some moisturizer onto his hands and spread it on one of her legs. Then he began rubbing, beginning at the knee and going way up the thigh before kneading his fingers into her muscles all the way down to her toes.

"Oh, my God. That feels so good. Finish up your workout and come upstairs quick. I need some more of that."

"I've been thinking about this stuff a lot lately because I want more for myself. And I want more for you too. So say no. If the Governor really wants you on his team, he'll have to offer you something bigger. If you say yes to an undercard position, you could get stuck there forever. You deserve more. You're special."

Luci closed the lotion bottle and placed it off to the side. Then she leaned back on her elbows and smiled. "You're special, Mark. Look where you are now. A job like this for you is once in a lifetime. So Johnson must think you're special too if he's even thinking about making you an advisor. Just promise me one thing."

"What's that?"

"Just never forget that I've known you were special for a long time. Everyone else—Johnson included—is late to the dance."

"I know that," he said as he leaned down and started kissing the side of her neck. "You don't have to keep reminding me. Or are you trying to say I owe you?" He alternated kissing and licking all the way down her leg to her bright red toenails.

Luci tried unsuccessfully to stifle a giggle. "That tickles. Stop."

"No." He continued down the other leg. This time, when he reached the bottom, he started gently sucking on her toes as he pressed both thumbs deep into the bottom of her foot, massaging back and forth. Luci arched her back and groaned out loud.

"Oh, my God, that feels so good. You're making me wet, Mark. Stop for a second and let's take this upstairs."

Mark stood upright and smiled as Luci regained her composure and pointed at him with both index fingers. "You get upstairs and get showered. I have some things I want you to do to me."

"Will I still respect myself in the morning?"

Luci rose to her feet, hooked her thumbs through the side strings of her underwear, and slowly rolled them down around her ankles until she could step out of them. She placed them in Mark's hand and bit him hard on the earlobe. Then she whispered into his ear.

"Not if you do it right. Let's go — I need you right now."

...

Mark was lying awake in bed with an arm around his sleeping wife. She was snoring quietly. He squeezed her tightly, kissed her on the forehead, and headed for the shower to rinse off and think.

He waited for the water to get hot, and the glass-encased shower began to fill with steam. Then he stood motionless under the shower head and let the hot water roll down his back. He stretched his muscles for several minutes before sitting down on the granite bench, leaning back against the tiled wall of their large custom master shower.

Agnes. She would have been proud of me.

Mark reached over to the controls, turned off the hot water, and turned on the cold full blast. He inhaled sharply as the freezing-cold water splashed against his skin. Then he took deep breaths, holding each one for several seconds and exhaling slowly until his body adjusted to the temperature.

Would she be proud of my accomplishments? Yes. Of my family? Yes. But she'd have a lot to say about my relationship with McDermott. My mother. Why do I have such a hard time saying those two words? My mother. Is it because she hasn't been completely honest?

Mark thought back to the heartfelt note Agnes had left behind for him in the event that she should die while he was away. In that letter, she had made the shocking and unanticipated revelation of the identity of Mark's birth mother. But the part of the letter that he had remembered most often was in her advice on how to live a meaningful life.

"At the end of your life, the only thing that matters is if you loved and allowed yourself to be loved." The first part is easy. How could anyone not love Luci and the kids? I could even learn to love McDermott, assuming that she had good reason to do what she did. But it's that second part I have difficulty with—allowing yourself to be loved. Sounds too much like submission—something I don't do well.

He stood up, changed the water temperature back to hot, and let the water hit him on the top of his head. He exhaled slowly until his lungs were completely empty, then paused for a four-count before inhaling slowly and deeply through his nostrils. The steam felt good.

As a career soldier and operator, Mark knew to leverage his advantages. Being the son of a sitting senator could certainly be an advantage if managed properly. Mark turned off the water and toweled off in front of the mirror. He could hear Dunbar's voice loud and clear in his mind: "Don't ever do anything unless you're sure you can sleep at night."

I'll sleep like a baby. By the time I'm done, everybody is going to get what they want. In exchange for her confirmation vote, McDermott gets to save a bunch of refugees. She ends up happy. Johnson's happy. I look like a hero and I get to reform the Family and operate without a leash. No more of this private security shit. No more being a mercenary. I'll serve the flag again instead of a logo.

He pulled on a pair of Red Sox boxer shorts and slid back into bed beside Luci. She was snoring louder than ever. He kissed her on the cheek and rolled over to face in the other direction.

Don't worry, Senator ... Mom. You'll get your moments in the public sun with the whole big happy family. Just not yet. You need to do some things for me first.

If you wanted to rob a bank you could use explosives to blow your way into the vault. It would be effective but very risky. To mitigate risk, you might instead focus on the bank manager who maintains the access codes. Then compel him to open the vault using force or deception. For example, you could break into his home and hold his family hostage while he opens the vault for you. Or you could trick him into opening it.

Let's just hope encouraging her to open the vault works. Because she's going to have to vote to confirm Judge Midas one way or another.

CHAPTER SIX: Heike

Mark scanned the streets repeatedly as he walked west on Boylston Avenue, his mind searching for an explanation of the meeting he was about to enter. Dunbar had been crystal-clear about the time and place. And although he named the foreign intelligence service Mark was to meet with, he didn't say a word about the topic to be discussed. In their sixty-second conversation, all Dunbar said was that it was somehow related to the dead Russian guy. Then he said he had to go and hung up.

Lately it's been impossible to get off the phone with the old man. He's rambled more in the past six months than in the previous six years. Now all of a sudden he's in a rush? Something's up.

Mark paused in front of the Boston Public Library and scanned the area with his peripheral vision. When an MBTA bus stopped to pick up passengers, he shuffled behind them at the end of the line as if he was going to board and then changed his mind at the last minute. He continued heading west on Boylston Street, doing a quick 360-degree scan to see if anyone appeared to have been thrown off by his sudden change of course.

Nothing. At least nobody stupid enough to follow me on foot. Especially right here.

He passed through the finish line area of the Boston Marathon and felt his pulse quicken.

Dirtbags.

He remembered being somewhere in Prague and hearing of the bombing first through a CNN "breaking news" alert on his phone. He remembered his initial reaction upon seeing pictures of the victims—a dangerous mix of heartbreak and rage—and completely losing it after seeing the beautiful young eight-year-old boy who had been robbed of his life. He thought of the young boy's smile and of his own two children, about to be tucked into their beds at home. He couldn't imagine a world without them. Then he recalled the younger terrorist brother on the cover of *Rolling Stone*. Quickly, Mark forced himself to think of something else lest he lose his mind.

Mark entered the historic Lenox Hotel and headed for the entry to City Bar, on the opposite side of the busy lobby. He glanced at his watch as he opened the door. Happy hour was just starting. He paused for a moment to let his eyes adjust to the new environment. Then he casually scanned the room from left to right before deciding on a space at the end of the bar, up against the wall.

Mark nodded hello to the bartender and, after quickly perusing the wine list, ordered a glass of Egon Muller Riesling from the Mosel region of Germany. This was one of the many German things for which he had acquired a taste over the years. German food, German history, even the German language had been such a large part of his life, thanks to his adopted mother Agnes's tutelage. He lifted the glass to his nose, breathed in deeply, and said a silent thank-you to Agnes for all she had done for him.

Mark sipped the sweet, dry Riesling and prepared for the crisp finish. The aroma of pears and apples filled his mouth and nostrils as he scanned the room again. He pulled up the sleeve of his tailored jacket and looked at the face of his watch on the inside of his left wrist.

Right place. Right time. Nobody I know from BND in sight. Not very German of you so far, mein freund.

The German BND, or *Bundesnachrichtendienst,* is the Republic of Germany's foreign intelligence service. Mark couldn't remember offhand the last time he'd had contact with anyone from the group, but he knew it had been a long time and was deeply curious why one of their guys would want a meeting with one of Dunbar's people so urgently. The only thing he knew for sure was that it must be important. Germans don't get on planes and fly across the Atlantic just to say hello.

New operators spend weeks or months learning the fundamentals of covert tradecraft. Then they spend the rest of their careers honing their instincts and perfecting the art. Good operators can blend in and make themselves less inconspicuous, but the best ones can dissolve by making themselves unremarkable in any way. As a result, they typically move through environments unnoticed—even under the noses of individuals who may be looking for them specifically. Operators at Mark's level have thus trained themselves to focus consciously on and give extra scrutiny to the seemingly unremarkable figures in their immediate surroundings. But nobody in the room seemed to warrant any special attention. All was quiet as Mark waited for his contact to arrive.

Like an 80s spy movie, Dunbar. Where is this guy? Who is this guy? And what does he want to sprechen *with me about?*

When she opened the door to the bar and stepped through the threshold, nobody seemed to pay much attention to the blonde-haired, green-eyed woman dressed in black from head to toe. But for Mark, it was as if a supernova had just exploded in the doorway. She glided toward Mark's position at the end of the bar, moving quickly yet gracefully, just fast enough to save time without drawing undue notice.

Heike? You gotta be kidding me. I did not see this coming.

She had a long black, cashmere winter coat draped over her arm and wore knee-high black leather boots. Her long blonde hair was weaved into a thick braid that hung down between her shoulder blades. She had smooth milky skin and wore almost no makeup. Age: mid-forties, with the athletic build of a former competitive athlete who kept herself in shape. A natural beauty.

Dangerous as hell, too.

"Mark," she said with a smile that started out chilly and ended lukewarm. "It's good to see you."

Mark pointed to the long coat folded over her arm. "Is that a Mauser under there or are you just happy to see me?"

She looked confused by the joke, so he moved on before things could get too awkward.

"It's good to see you too, Heike. Long time."

"Ja, long time, Mark." She pointed at his glass. "Let me guess— a Riesling?"

"I'm impressed. You remember. Indeed, it is." He motioned to the bartender to bring one for the lady. She placed her coat at the bar in front of them and scanned the room as she spoke.

"How long has it been, Mark? Some years now, yes? Maybe nine or ten since Berlin?"

"Something like that. A long time, regardless. Where are you now? Still in Munich?"

She nodded thanks to the bartender and picked up her glass. "Not anymore. I was transferred back home to Berlin this past year. And it's very good to be home. To home, Mark. *Prost.*" She raised her glass.

"*Prost,*" replied Mark.

They touched glasses and looked each other in the eyes. Her eyes were as green as the emerald in Luci's engagement ring. She licked her lips and smiled. He had forgotten how stunning she was when she let the light shine through. She looked him over quickly and the smile evaporated.

"Well, I had always wondered if someone had made an honest man out of you yet. Now I know. You are obviously spoken for now, *ja?*"

Mark glanced at the wedding ring on his left hand. "Yes, married now. About five years."

Her smile returned as she laughed. "I wasn't talking about the ring, Mark, but about the rather obvious fact that someone else—a very beautiful, intelligent woman, I presume—is laying your clothes out on the bed for you in the morning. *Ja?*"

Mark looked down at himself. He tried not to blush, but she was right. The outfit and watch he was wearing cost more than his entire wardrobe, plus the car he was driving, when he first met Heike in Berlin. Thanks to private-sector pay and Luci's tastes, his days of walking into a room underdressed were over. And although he hated to admit it, he had no desire to return to the old Mark.

"*Sie haben kinder?*" she asked.

"*Zwillinge.*"

"Twins! *Herzlichen Glückwunsch*, Mark. I am very happy for you. And I am not surprised. You always were … *spezielle.*" She placed her hand flat on his upper pectoral region and pressed down gently. Then she let her hand drop and brush across the tip of his nipple on its way back to her glass. He kept his poker face, but she could see his chest rise as he inhaled. He wasn't sure if it had been intentional or not.

Is this really happening? I thought I'd never see her again. Where's my glass?

. . .

"And so that is why I am here, Mark. Just for you. We wanted you to know that before we talk, *ja? Verstehst du?*"

"*Ja, ja, ja. Ich verstehe.*" It had not taken her long, but it still annoyed him how she chose to begin the conversation.

Yeah, Heike. You normally wouldn't even talk to someone in the private security sector. You're doing me some kind of huge favor. Got it. Now why the hell are you here?

"I am here—we, your German friends, are here—because of our history together. Not just you and I personally"—she paused long enough to make it awkward—"but our two countries. We, as you say, go back a long way, and if you cannot count on your friends, then who can you count on?"

"Agreed."

Heike leaned in closer and lowered her voice. "The unidentified man in Boston from your recent incident is—"

"Oh, you mean Dmitri?"

Heike paused. *"Ja,* Dmitri. *Ser gut.* Honestly, I might have thought less of you if you hadn't gotten at least that far. Shall I continue?"

Mark nodded.

"Then you know he is a lifelong thug in the Russian criminal underground. He used to work for a man in western Russia. A man named Boris Popov who—"

"Yes, I know. Evidently, this Boris guy got whacked a few years ago."

Heike rolled her eyes and finished off her Riesling. "Perhaps I am wasting your time, Mark."

"Not at all, Heike. You just haven't told me anything I didn't already know yet."

"I can see that. *Vielen dank* for the wine. It was nice to see you. Best of luck. I imagine you already know everything there is to know about the man in the white hat, so I won't waste any of your time talking about him."

She retrieved her coat from the bar and turned to exit. Mark gently clasped her by the elbow and pointed to his glass. "I love this Riesling too much to drink it alone, and I like hearing you talk. If I order a bottle, will you help me with it?" He smiled warmly and pretended not to be scanning the room though knowing full well that she was too skilled an operator not to notice.

Heike threw her head back and stifled a laugh. "Not bad, Mark. Not bad at all. You are still charming. But you are also so ..."

"So *what?*"

"Amerikan." She said it with a playful snarl that transported Mark back in time.

Images began flashing in his mind. Berlin. Reichstag. The ruins of an insidious wall that divided a common people. Standing side by side with her in front of the Brandenburg Gate. Late at night. Flashes of pink neon disco lights and a chest-thumping bass loud enough to rattle the windows a block away. Closing time. Heike on top, riding like crazy while gazing down at him with those sparkling emerald eyes and the same snarl on her face.

Mark laughed. "I'll take that as a compliment." He moved closer and placed his hand on her waist. "And I was serious. Would you like another?"

She looked into his brown eyes and took a deep breath to offset her rising heartbeat. "No, *danke*. I have a plane to catch. I'm in and out, Mark. Back to Berlin tonight."

He said nothing and waited. She continued after several seconds of silence.

"It's funny, you know. You are definitely American, Mark Landry. But I think you must have some German in you as well. The best of both worlds, *ja?*"

Mark stood a bit straighter, nodded his head, and glanced at the clock mounted on the wall behind the bar. She sensed his impatience, glanced at her own watch, and got to the chase.

"Your man in the white hat is Oleg Borodin. A Russian FSB operative recently assigned to the embassy in D.C. under official cover as a low-level bureaucrat. Thoroughly boring at first glance, but in quite deep, actually."

"Quite deep? FSB or Russian Mafia?"

"What's the difference these days, Mark?"

"Good point. What else have you got?"

"We believe he is directing significant networks of criminals, hackers, and intelligence operatives within your country. Significant, Mark."

"Okay. What exactly is he directing them to do?"

"Disrupt. Confuse. Classic Soviet-style *dezinformatsiya*. Create problems where none existed and then exacerbate those problems. Infiltrate various movements like your militia movement and encourage violence. International sanctions have squeezed the Russian economy so badly the Kremlin is doubling its espionage efforts abroad."

"What do you have to back all of that up?"

"Some files for you and your analysts to look at. We are confident they contain detailed proof of Borodin's network in the United States and Europe. Some parts are readable, but most of the files are encrypted and we have been unable to break in. If you find anything of value, please remember where it came from and keep us informed. Now, I really must go. My plane is ready for the return trip and we have much to worry about in Berlin these days."

Mark had a feeling that she was giving him the information partially because of their history together. But Heike also knew that giving the data directly to an official U.S. intelligence organization might raise questions about the extent of Germany's intelligence operations within the United States. She was playing it safe by handing the file over to Mark. She and the BND trusted his discretion on what information to share and with whom. He had earned that trust by putting his life on the line in Berlin almost a decade earlier.

"I'll keep you out of this. I appreciate it, Heike. And best of luck back home. Let me know if I can ever return the favor."

"You are much better off here, Mark. One can drive from Damascus to Germany. Therefore, we must simultaneously deal with jihadists as well as Russian aggression. Your country is blessed by geography, yet you still spend most of your time chasing the ghost of bin Laden." She reached into the front pocket of her slim-fitting black slacks. She was beginning her exfiltration.

"Meanwhile," she continued, "a foreign state power – Russian power – festers from within. Your countrymen need to wake up. Winter isn't coming, Mark. It is already here."

Mark helped Heike to put her coat on. She leaned in close and gently kissed him on the side of the cheek while reaching around with one hand. Placing the palm of her hand flat on his rear end, she pushed the digital files into his back pocket with her thumb. He caught a whiff of her perfume and felt himself teetering on the edge of arousal.

He watched Heike walk toward the door with the confidence of a European runway model. He could feel something and he wondered if she felt it too. She paused in the doorway and turned back to see if he was still looking. Then she walked across the lobby of the Lenox Hotel with a smile on her face.

Mark pulled the phone from his front pocket and sent an early warning message to Imperium analysts that raw data relating to the dead guy, Dmitri, and the guy in the white hat, Oleg Borodin, were on the way. He paid the bill and breathed in the fresh air after exiting through one of the hotel's side doors. A hint of Heike's perfume remained in his nostrils.

He thought about her on the walk back down Boylston Avenue to his car.

They could have shared the information through a number of different intermediaries, but they chose me. They could have sent anybody, but they sent her. I don't believe in coincidences. Something tells me I'm going to see her again.

Mark started up the Range Rover and pulled into Boston traffic.

The phone resting between his legs started to vibrate. It was Luci.

"Are you alone? I got another offer today that I wanted to run by you," asked Luci.

"Me? Yeah, I'm alone. Why? Who would I be with?" Mark turned the corner and headed east on Boylston Street. "Go ahead. I'm on my way back to the Game Room. Tell me, who wants you on their team now?"

. . .

Kenny and several other analysts and cyber-operators were already gathered around a workstation examining the data dump within minutes of Mark's arrival back at Imperium. He tapped Kenny on the shoulder and motioned for him to come into Mark's office.

"I know what you're going to say, Mark."

"No, you don't."

"Yeah, I do. You want me to go home and rest. But honestly, I feel a lot better and can't stand being at home, especially when I feel responsible."

"Kenny, I have no idea why you are here. But this is important stuff and you're a big boy, so I'm not going to send you packing. But I do expect you to take care of yourself. Moreover, I want to dispel any thoughts in that head of yours that you are responsible for what happened. You're not. You just had extremely bad luck. It happens to the best. That's it. Feel free to jump back into the mix out there. I want an update from someone as soon as you guys know anything."

Mark watched Kenny exit and knew how he must be feeling. On what was to be the most exciting night of his life, he got blindsided and his whole world was turned upside down. Now he wanted to do whatever it took to make things right. And his technical expertise was certainly needed by the rest of the Imperium team.

Mark hoped that Heike's files would bear fruit and explain Oleg Borodin's network of operatives the Germans were so convinced was operating in the U.S. There was always talk of active Russian spies and espionage, but Mark had yet to see much hard evidence to back it up.

Why would someone who had to know there was a high probability of surveillance meet with an idiot like Dmitri? Unless Heike was right. Maybe the FBI and other American intel assets were too tied up and focused on stopping the next lone wolf to properly track more sophisticated threats like Oleg Borodin.

Mark saw Senator McDermott on CNN and turned up the volume. They were showing a clip from her interview earlier that evening. Obviously they had already reported on her recent trip to the refugee camp.

"May I ask one more question, Senator? We have only a minute or so left," asked Anderson Cooper.

"Shoot."

"With the House currently more evenly divided between parties than the Senate, there have been some encouraging signs that people are talking across the aisle on the House side, as well as having meaningful dialogue within factions of each caucus. Are you hopeful at all that the Senate will become more open to debate, instead of less open to any debate at all as it has been in recent years?"

McDermott spoke confidently with a smile on her face. Her words were clear, her delivery well-honed through thousands of similar interviews. She had certainly stumbled and fallen a few times in the early years of her public life, but each time she had gotten up and marched forward. The result was her cool-as-a-cucumber vibe even during heated discussions.

"Anderson, the House isn't exactly a utopia of bipartisanship, but I get your point. They have much more diversity of opinion on policy. Meanwhile, the Senate has 59 Republicans, 40 Democrats, and 1 independent who tends to vote with Democrats. And so deadlock is the default position in the Senate these days. When will it end? When the voters decided it must end. It's that simple. Term limits aren't a viable option. The only thing we can do is vote and continue hoping for a better Senate."

"But that sounds so defeatist, with all due respect, Senator. Do you really have such little confidence that senators will ever break with their party on the big votes like Supreme Court justices or Cabinet members? Judge James Midas has been waiting 200 days for a vote. Is that right?"

"Look," she said. "On some of the smaller things, I think we can find common ground. But when it comes to things like Supreme Court justices I do worry. The two parties have very different visions for America, and confirming justices is arguably the most significant thing we are called upon to do as senators. So I don't envision much progress there. But some of the more day-to-day governing doesn't have to be quite so contentious."

"Thank you, Senator McDermott of Connecticut, member of the Senate Select Committee on Intelligence and frequent visitor to our studios."

Mark pulled out his phone and texted McDermott.

MARK: You in town tomorrow?

He put the phone down on his desk. An analyst knocked twice on the door on his way into the office.

"Have you got anything?"

"Kind of, but not really. There a ton of data here. Some of the files we can read. Names, places. Other parts are unreadable, and most are encrypted. We're trying to get in now through brute force. It could be a while, or never. There's no way to tell yet, but I'll let you know as soon as anything changes."

Mark leaned to the side and looked out into the Game Room through his office door. Kenny was slumped over a laptop, his one good eye focused on the monitor, doing his best to type, then scanning through pictures of Dmitri's Venezuelan passport.

Is this a real passport? If so, it had to cost a fortune. Where and when was it issued?

"Hey, new guy," Kenny said waving to one of the newer, younger cyber-operators. "What's your name?"

"Thomas."

"Do me a favor, will you, Thomas? See this passport? Find out when it was issued. All it says is the year. I want the date. Also see if it's ever been used. Talk to the other guys. Ask around. Get creative. Just get the answer to the question as soon as humanly possible."

Kenny sent an encrypted message to Patty:

KENNY: Hey, I'm feeling better. Would like to hear your voice. Are you home or at work? Can you give me a secure call?
PATTY: Home. Sure. 10 min.

Back in his office, Mark tapped the analyst on the shoulder and pointed to Kenny. "I need to get on a plane. Keep an eye on him. If he goes anywhere, David will be with him. But if he looks like he's struggling, let me know. He looks better, but he did get a pretty good thumping."

"Will do."

The analyst exited. Mark's phone vibrated. McDermott had responded to his text.

MCDERMOTT: Yes. Committee hearings midday. Otherwise free.

He slipped the phone back into his front pocket.

Then I guess I'll be seeing you bright and early, Senator. We've got a Supreme Court nominee to get behind and not much time to do it.

CHAPTER SEVEN: Prodigal Son

Senator McDermott tapped the off button on her alarm clock and splashed cold water on her face before returning to grab her phone from the night stand. The apartment's automatic lights clicked on as she made her way down the hall toward the kitchen.

She removed a half-eaten yogurt from the refrigerator and rinsed off a spoon in the sink. A gentle ding indicated that her morning coffee was ready. She sipped it as she scrolled through her messages. The phone gently vibrated in her hand, indicating the arrival of a new text. She opened it and froze in disbelief.

MARK: I'm in town. Up for coffee this morning? Or are you busy?

Coffee? My son is asking me to coffee. Not calling to talk about my Imperium security detail. Not texting just to make sure I'm breathing. He actually wants to sit and talk. Or is this too good to be true?

MCDERMOTT: Sure! Still open till noon.

Her assistant answered her phone on the first ring.

"Good morning, Senator."

"Good morning, Christie. Do me a favor and cancel my morning. I'll be in for hearings later, but something has come up."

"Okay. Is everything all right, Ma'am?"

"Never been better. See you at—"

"Senator, wait. Remember, you've been forgetting things lately. Important things. So I just want to confirm that you want me to cancel your entire morning—including your nine o'clock appointment with—"

"Don't worry about it, Christie. Cancel it. I'll see you at noon."

She dropped her phone on the sofa and walked back down the hall, whistling and clapping her hands to the imaginary beat in her head.

My son and I are having coffee. My son and I are having coffee.

. . .

"I'm coming. I'm coming. Hold your horses!" McDermott called out over her shoulder. She searched for a set of matching earrings in the pile of jewelry on her bathroom counter. Then she put on a touch of mascara, blush, and lipstick. The doorbell sounded for the fourth time.

"I'd better have won Publishers' Clearing House or something! Seriously, where's the fire?" she said, approaching the door and turning the knob. "I wonder what my crack Imperium security team is doing right now."

She opened the door and froze in disbelief again.

"Sorry, I guess I could come back if this is a bad time," said Mark, with his hands in the front pockets of his windbreaker. He had a baseball cap with the Imperium logo pulled down over his head and a smile from ear to ear.

She smiled back, bowed her head, and laughed.

"Sorry, Mark. I can be a bear in the morning. But I'm glad you're here. Come on in."

"Actually, I'm going to wait down in the garage. Whenever you're ready, we can head out and grab a cup of coffee wherever you want. Unless you'd prefer to just stay here?"

She stared at him speechless for several seconds, her eyes wide.

My son wants to have coffee with me ... in public. In public. Am I dreaming?

"Okay, sure. I know a place where folks like me can go without too much of a hassle. I'll be right down."

Mark gave two thumbs up and smiled. "Great. I'll see you at the car. And don't forget your license."

"My license? Why?"

"You're driving."

...

"It's just a few more blocks up on the right. There's a spot for us, but I don't know what the rest of the security detail will do. Where are they anyway? I don't see anybody. Do you think I lost them?"

Mark tried unsuccessfully to keep from laughing. Then he turned and leaned in closer to his mother. "Absolutely. After all, you are a member of the Senate Select Committee on Intelligence, right? Their skills were no match for yours."

She nodded at his sarcasm, happy to be having a playful back-and-forth with her son. "Of course I'm joking. And although I don't always see them, I know they are always there. It's comforting, even if it is sort of creepy at times."

"Yeah, well, you're safe with Sadie's team. That's all that matters. So you can focus more on doing your job and living your life. Trust me. If her team can't protect you, nobody can."

She nodded and turned right onto a narrow side street in the Georgetown area of Washington. Mark scanned the area as she put the car into park and turned it off.

"That was the first time I have driven in the past few years. I really needed that. Thanks, Mark."

"No problem. But I'll be driving back. It's too dangerous to have a senator behind the wheel. Too many things can go wrong."

"Nice of you to tell me that now," she said with a smile.

Mark stepped onto the sidewalk and gently guided her by the right arm toward the café entrance. "I told Sadie's team to take the day off and brought a team of my own instead. I told them in advance you'd be driving. They had you bumper-locked the whole way here. There's still always a risk, but in this case it was minimal. Besides, it was worth it."

"Really? What made it worth it?"

"You got to be normal for a few minutes. And I got to see you smile."

She stepped inside, nodded to the owner and a few patrons and headed directly to a small, private table in the back corner. It was surrounded by bookshelves to give its occupants privacy.

Me, normal? He liked seeing me smile? Is this really happening?

Mark's team had already cleared the café for surveillance prior to their arrival. If she hadn't chosen that particular café, Mark would have chosen it for her.

. . .

"Okay, but this is the last one, though. I always swore I wouldn't be one of those people constantly flashing pictures of their kids. Then I became a father and that went right out the window."

Mark scrolled through the photo stream on his phone and tapped twice on the one he was looking for. "The kids used every piece of tape in the house to get the blankets to stay in place just long enough to call it Fort Landry. Then our dog Murphy tore the whole thing down."

McDermott took the phone into her hands. "Awww, that's so cute. They must love having that dog around. Not bad work on the fort either."

"It's in their blood. I made a lot of forts in the living room when I was a kid. But I was usually alone. No siblings, no dog. It is nice that they have each other."

She faked a smile and looked down into her empty coffee mug. He immediately regretted his word choice.

Why did you have to point that out? She knows you grew up an only child, asshole. You're here to build trust and dangle the relationship she wants with you and the family, not make her feel shitty about giving you up for adoption. Recover.

"Hey, I've been meaning to ask you something."

"What's that?"

"I caught the last time you were on with Anderson Cooper, and there was a part at the beginning where it looked like you were about to burst out laughing. You caught yourself in time, but there was a split second where I could see something was tearing you up. Am I wrong?"

McDermott sat back in her chair and folded her arms across her chest. "Wow. I'm impressed. How did you catch that?"

"Dunno. Just happened to look at the right time, I guess. What was so funny?"

She overemphasized cocking her head from side to side as if to check for eavesdroppers and held an index finger to her lips. "Since you paid for the coffees, I will tell you, but you are sworn to secrecy."

Mark stared at her expressionless, waiting for her to proceed.

"Do you promise? I'm not sharing until I have your word."

He rolled his eyes and raised two fingers. "Scout's honor."

"Okay. It goes back to my first days in the Senate when Megan and I were working side by side every day trying to figure things out. And I have to give full credit to ... her."

Your sister. Do you know how bad I want to say that—"your sister"? Or how badly I want to see you all in the same room at least once in my life?

"Anyway, Cooper asked me something about House Republicans, but every time I hear those two words I think of Megan's name for them. She used to call them the tighty whitey brigade. It's silly, I know. But it was funny at the time and just kind of stuck."

"That's it? You almost lost it over that? I mean, I guess it's kinda funny."

"It was funny the way she said it. She can be hilarious at all the wrong moments. I miss having her around."

"At least you got to see her at the refugee camp. She won't be there forever. Which is good, because I'd like to meet her one day. Eventually she'll come back to the states or at least move on to somewhere safer. I wouldn't worry about her too much, though. Imperium would never have taken you there if it weren't at least somewhat safe. We never would have taken the risk."

Did he just say he wanted to meet his sister one day? Wow.

McDermott pointed at Mark's hat. "Speaking of Imperium, I like the logo. There's something about it that grabs my attention, but I can't put my finger on it. Maybe it's the emerald green stone. I've always loved that color."

"You have a good eye. That was my only input. It's inspired by Agnes's emerald ring. She gave it to me and I gave it to Luci instead of a diamond when we got engaged. Ask her to see it next time we're all together. It's striking when you hold it up to the light."

McDermott smiled and nodded.

The next time we're together? So this coffee isn't just a one-off?

"Agnes was the best mother anyone could have asked for. I'm not sure if I ever told you that, but I wanted you to know you left me in good hands. She was one of a kind and I miss her."

McDermott didn't know what to make of everything. This was the longest, deepest conversation they had had since their first reunion five years earlier. It was a lot to process. She looked slightly uncomfortable. Mark continued before she could say anything.

"I'm sorry if that came out awkward. She was a great woman. I said it because I want you to feel good about your decision, not regretful. I had a great childhood and never once felt abandoned. There were times when I would lay awake wondering who you were, where you were, and whether you ever thought about me. Sometimes I wondered what your hair smelled like or how your laugh sounded. But I never once questioned your decision."

McDermott started to tear up, so she removed the napkin wrapped around her coffee cup and dabbed the corners of her eyes with it. Mark continued in a low, steady, almost hypnotic tone. She focused all her attention on the words coming slowly out of his mouth.

"And I know I've never said this before, but I've been thinking a lot lately and I feel like I need to thank you."

"Thank me? For what, Mark? You have nothing to thank me for."

"Yes, I do. You gave me my life. You had a choice. And you chose to give me my life."

She quickly pulled another napkin to her face. Mark caught a glimpse of her reaction before she was able to cover her face.

What was that? Pure shock. Why? Maybe she didn't choose to have me. Maybe she was compelled to carry me and give me up for adoption. Or is she just emotional about the new warmth and prospect of a closer relationship with me?

McDermott tried unsuccessfully to hold back the tears. "Oh, Mark. You don't have anything to thank me for. I'm looking at you right now and I couldn't be happier. You and your whole family are any mother's dream. An absolute dream."

Mark looked around to make sure they were still alone. If anyone had seen them together, it wouldn't be a big deal. She was simply a senator having coffee with the head of her security detail. That's why he wore the windbreaker and Imperium cap. But if she were crying, someone might get nosy.

"What do you say we get out of here so we can both get some work done?"

"Good idea. I'll just visit the ladies' room quickly. Be right back."

Mark watched her walk confidently across the café toward the bathrooms. So far, things were going perfectly. She had been receptive to his newfound warmth. Shocked, but receptive. But there was something peculiar about her reaction to his gratitude for choosing to give birth to him. He reviewed his progress thus far while scrolling through his new messages.

She wasn't expecting any of this when she got up this morning. She's still processing it all. Don't feel bad. It's not like you're lying. It's all true. And you would have eventually said all these things anyway. You're just speeding up the timeline a little bit so you can get some things done. Besides, she lied to you first.

He could hear footsteps approaching the table and looked up to see her refreshed and beaming from within. "Do you have plans for dinner tonight?"

"Me? No. No plans," Mark answered, smiling up at his mother.

"Me neither. Would you like to join me? I have committee meetings all afternoon and early evening. But after that I'll be home all night. I just have to warn you, I'm a terrible cook."

"So am I," he answered, getting up from the table. "Maybe I get it from you. Or maybe I got it from Teddy. Was he a good cook?"

"I never got the chance to find out." She smiled and looked down at the phone in her hands as she answered. "But one thing I do know is that I need to get back to my office before my staff has a hissy fit. I told them to cancel my morning, which they did. But I forgot I had another meeting off the books that they didn't know about until he showed up. Now they're panicking and the press is asking questions. Seriously, don't people have bigger things to worry about?"

Mark gently placed his left hand on the small of his mother's back and escorted her toward the door with a smile on his face. He glanced around and wondered how many lawmakers and staffers frequented places like these and connected to the public wifi network while there, unaware of the tremendous damage someone like Kenny could do to them. Then he refocused his attention on his mother.

"Why is your staff so mad? Who'd you blow off?"

"James Midas. The Supreme Court nominee."

. . .

"What's this guy's name again?" Mark pointed to the photograph sitting atop several stacks of papers that McDermott had pushed to the other side of the kitchen table to make room for the Chinese food.

"Ahab. I have no idea why but that's what everyone calls him. We're working on a real name—or I'm told somebody is working on it. He's one of the bigger human traffickers taking advantage of the situation. The stories are horrifying. What this guy does to women and children—he needs to be stopped."

Mark chewed on a mouthful of pork fried rice and examined the picture.

"How do you propose stopping him?"

"Once we get confirmation on his identity, we will issue an Interpol warrant. Maybe offer a reward. And he will be brought to justice."

"A warrant? That's sure to have him shaking in his boots." Mark lifted his chopsticks and swallowed a mouthful of noodles, then washed it down with a gulp of cold beer. "Sorry to be sarcastic, but I've dealt with guys like this before. They don't think like us. How do you rate the chances of him being brought to justice because of a warrant?"

"I don't know and it doesn't really matter. I can't control the outcome, but I still have to do everything I can to help. I made a promise to Asha." McDermott rummaged through the papers on the table looking for the picture. "Here she is. You should have seen how hopeful she looked after we spoke. Her story was bad enough—you heard it. But the kids. The orphans. Nobody really has a firm count, but we're talking six figures. Children either running for their lives or living in a camp surrounded by barbed wire and armed guards. And we're doing nothing to help."

"It's not that easy. Guys like this Ahab character don't get scared unless they think someone is going to show up on their doorstep. Everything else is just paper."

"Are you saying the problem can't be solved?"

"Not at all. But to solve that particular problem, you'd have to go in the way Pompey the Great did for Rome."

"How's that?"

"Unrestrained."

"Unrestrained?"

"Exactly. You wouldn't even have to get to each and every smuggler and pirate. You'd just have to hit a few of them hard enough to put the fear of God in the rest of them. People like that thrive on the fact that everyone else is afraid of them. Going at them tenfold is the only thing that'll get their attention. It's effective, but not pretty."

"It doesn't sound legal either. I'll just let the warrant work its way through the system and go from there. I need to concentrate on getting some relief for these refugees."

"So have you proposed some solutions that I just haven't heard about?"

"I've been trying, but it's impossible to get any real traction on anything concerning refugees. Nobody will even listen. It's frustrating, but this is a nut I am determined to crack."

"I'm not surprised. You've always had a thing for women and children's issues—just like Luci. It's noble. I respect that about you."

"Yeah, well, I appreciate that, but your sis—I mean, Megan, would beg to differ. I've done lots of talking and demonstrating and protesting, but I haven't made any tangible, measurable progress. That's one of the reasons she left. I can't say I blame her."

Mark grabbed a cold beer from the refrigerator.

"Split this with me," he said as he poured the first half of the bottle into McDermott's mug. "Everything in the Senate moves at a glacial pace. What was she expecting?"

"That doesn't matter now. The past is the past. I just have to figure out how to deliver on my promise to help."

Mark helped to clear the table when they had finished eating.

"Just throw those anywhere on the counter, Mark. I'll get to them later."

"Hey, I meant to ask you. What was up with your meeting with James Midas this morning? Did you really blow him off to have coffee with me? Or did you forget about the meeting?"

McDermott finished her beer, smiled, and rinsed the glass out under the kitchen faucet. "I forgot about everything as soon as I got your text. And I wouldn't change today if I could. I got to spend time with you, which is always special. And I didn't waste any time by meeting with a judge I could never vote to confirm. I just don't see the point. Evidently a good number of my colleagues on the other side of the aisle disagree, but they'll get over it. It's been over two hundred days since the President nominated him. He should take the hint and nominate someone else because James Midas will never be confirmed to the Supreme Court."

"Sounds like you've definitely made up your mind."

"Have you seen the videos or read the transcripts from speeches he used to make before he became a judge? They're pretty hard to forget." She stuck her fork into the container of boneless spare ribs and fished around for a small one. "Have you read his book? 'The greatest threat to American democracy is the American left.' I believe that's a direct quote."

"Didn't he write that a long time ago?"

"Yes, but he was still a grown man at the time. He never should have made it to the bench in the first place—any bench. What about a case early in his career as a judge where he gave a group of young men a collective slap on the wrist for sexual assault, felt the need to shame the victims for their 'poor judgment,' and wondered aloud why they agreed to return to the fraternity house in the first place? Because, you know, if you don't want to be assaulted, you shouldn't go to parties, right? That's just the tip of the iceberg. He'd overturn *Roe v. Wade* the first chance he gets. The National Organization of Women, ACLU, and countless other organizations have condemned his nomination. But he does have a 100% approval rating from the NRA."

"I'm sensing you don't like him very much."

"It's not about liking him or not. It's about whether I think he'd make a suitable Supreme Court justice. And I find him unsuitable for the aforementioned reasons."

"Okay, I was just curious. Personally, I don't think it would be the end of the world if he got confirmed. I don't know of anyone who wouldn't go back and change some of the things they've done or said in their lives if they could. Regardless, at least your position is based on principle and not just reelection politics."

"It's all principle. Any I'm not running for reelection."

Did she just say she's not running for reelection?

"Really? Wow? How is that not breaking news?"

"Because I haven't announced it. You're the only person I've told."

"May I ask why?"

"I want to move on and do other things. I want to focus more on specific projects and causes. I want to be able to quantify whether or not I'm actually making a difference. Somebody else can play the long game in the U.S. Senate. I want to roll up my sleeves and get my hands dirty doing something worthwhile while I still can. With the people I care about most."

That means you and your family. If you'll just invite me in, Mark.

"Anyway, I'm sorry to get political. My views are out there for the universe to dissect. But you and I have never really talked about politics, so I don't know where you stand on things. And I don't want to assume anything."

"There's nothing to assume. This is going to sound weird, but I never voted until after I retired from service. For me, it would have been too difficult to separate the two. I never wanted to be in a position where I was saluting someone I didn't vote for. So I stayed out of it. It was easier that way."

Mark pulled on his windbreaker and scrolled though several messages on his phone. If he didn't call Doc soon, he would be in the doghouse with both Doc and Luci. "I need to do a few things before I go back to Boston tomorrow morning. So I'm going to head out. Thank you for dinner. This was nice. Thanks for taking the time."

"Thank you for coffee this morning and for coming tonight. This was a lot of fun. You're welcome here any time."

"I appreciate that. Luci does too. And if you ever need someone to talk to about anything, call me. It's got to be tough with Megan so far away."

"I may just take you up on that."

McDermott hugged Mark. He hugged her back, kissed her on the side of the head, and patted her on the back.

"Please do."

...

McDermott closed the door and locked it. Then she looked at the pile of files and reports with which she was supposed to familiarize herself for the following day's committee hearings. She decided to put them off until morning and changed into pajamas instead.

"Alexa, play the last song again."

A moment later, music from speakers mounted throughout the apartment began to fill the room. McDermott threw away the empty Chinese food containers and started wiping down the table and countertops.

Desperado, why don't you come to your senses?
You been out ridin' fences for so long now
Oh, you're a hard one
I know that you got your reasons
These things that are pleasin' you
Can hurt you somehow

What had started out as a typical day for McDermott had ended as one of the best of her life. She had spent almost an entire day with her son, who had been warm, charming, and open. And she wouldn't trade it for anything. But she had so many burning questions that she dared not ask for fear of pushing him away or—worse—opening the door for his burning questions, some of which she was still not ready for.

What did he mean when he said he had dealt with people like Ahab before? Where? Why? What did he do to them? She could trace Mark's Army career from enlistment through twelve years in the 75th Ranger Regiment. But after that, the paper trail went dry until he retired eight years later as a master sergeant. What was he doing during those last eight years of service? Out of habit, Mark downplayed his military career and experiences. But how was she not supposed to notice the way he calmly walked back into her life one night via her sixth-floor balcony?

Desperado, oh, you ain't gettin' no younger
Your pain and your hunger, they're drivin' you home
And freedom, oh freedom, well, that's just some people talkin'
Your prison is walking through this world all alone

She walked into the master bathroom, where she washed her face, brushed her teeth, and flossed. Those lifelong nightly rituals were the easy ones to remember. But since her number of prescriptions had recently gone from three to five, she needed the dosage schedule taped to the vanity mirror.

Don't your feet get cold in the winter time?
The sky won't snow and the sun won't shine
It's hard to tell the night time from the day
You're losin' all your highs and lows
Ain't it funny how the feeling goes away?

McDermott poured a glass of water and alternated between taking tiny sips and swallowing until she had taken all her medications. Then she added an Ambien on top of it to help her get to sleep. She pulled the decorative pillows off the bed and threw them into a pile on the floor. Then she drew back the comforter and snuggled in for the night as usual—alone.

Desperado, why don't you come to your senses?
Come down from your fences, open the gate
It may be rainin', but there's a rainbow above you
You better let somebody love you (let somebody love you)
You better let somebody love you before it's too late

She interlaced her fingers and brought them against her chin in prayer. Then she reflected on the extraordinary events of the day—an experience she had thought impossible just yesterday. They gave her hope for a possible tomorrow with Megan, Mark, Luci, and the twins in one room, as a family—the only thing that really matters.

Dear God, I would do anything to make that happen. Anything.

"Alexa, wake me up at 5 a.m."

. . .

Mark got into his vehicle and pulled out of McDermott's parking garage. He scrolled through his phone and saw at least three texts from Doc that had arrived during his dinner with his mother. He replied that he would call as soon as he got back to his hotel room.

Forty-five minutes later, Mark took off his shoes and shirt and splashed cold water on his face. He picked up his cell phone to call Doc. He looked through the minibar selection after dialing and opened a bottle of Riesling as Doc answered.

"Be still, my heart. If it isn't Mark Landry calling back finally. I was beginning to think I was off your Christmas card list."

"Not at all, Doc. Just taking care of business on this end and trying to give you some space on yours. How is she?"

"The same. How are you doing, Mark?" It was obvious from his quick response, redirecting the topic of discussion back to Mark, that Doc didn't want to talk about his dying wife.

"Never been better," Mark answered before looking at his watch and swallowing a mouthful of Riesling. "I'm in D.C. where apparently rush hour never ends."

"Why have you been avoiding me, Mark? Is everything okay?"

"Yeah. Everything is fine. Honestly, I really haven't been avoiding you—I've just been swamped. I don't know if Dunbar told you, but he—"

Doc cut him off. "I know. He's turning Imperium over to you. I'm happy for you. If that's what you want."

"Here we go. What's that supposed to mean? Of course it's what I want. You know that. And I'm throwing everything I have into it to make it work."

"Like you do everything, Mark. There's no doubt you'll be successful. Just remember that now you have the whole team depending on you being present and clear-headed at all times. So don't blow me off anymore, okay?"

"Understood."

"Good. Let's save time with the small talk and jump right into it. Are you still having the dreams?"

"Not really."

"When was the last dream?"

"At least a month ago." Mark swigged the rest of his wine and poured another glass.

"Tell me about it."

Mark paced to the window and looked out over the Capitol skyline. "The usual. Nothing different. Same dream I've been having for—what is it now? Two years?"

"Three. And we've talked about this, Mark. That's not an answer. Describe it for me. You have to verbalize it."

The dream opened the same way each time, with Mark sprinting up the driveway of Father Peck's parish in the middle of the night. He entered the church through the back door and descended the narrow concrete steps into the Dungeon. Father Peck was standing in the middle of the room, waiting for him.

"Expressionless. He's just standing there staring at me, but he never says a word. He looks like he wants to say something but he never does. I scream and yell. I jump up and down. I know he hears and sees me because the eye contact is so intense. But still he just stands there and says nothing. That goes on until I feel like I'm stuck in Jello and can't even move. I'm just stuck there with him looking at me and saying nothing. Then I wake up pissed off. That's it."

"What do you think it means, Mark?"

Mark laid down on his back and stared at the ceiling. "I have no idea. Probably nothing. I've tried, Doc. I really have. But sometimes a dream is just a dream."

"Not the persistent ones, Mark. There's often an underlying cause or message. How is everything else? Have you experienced any of the feelings I asked you to track?"

"Doc, no, I don't have time to be depressed—my kids won't let me. And no, I haven't been angry very often lately—only when Russian mobsters try to kill one of my people. What's the other big one? Guilt. Yeah, that was it. No, I don't feel guilty for anything I've done. Seriously, I appreciate your concern, but I've never been better. I've never felt better. And I wouldn't lie to you."

"I know that. Just promise me you'll keep me in the loop, okay?"

"You bet. Now I need some beauty rest. I fly to Palm Springs in the morning for some golf outing."

"Since when do you golf?"

"I didn't say I was playing."

. . .

"Look on the bright side," said the President. "This is the last key leader retreat you'll need to attend."

Senator Johnson stood on the eighteenth tee box with one hand resting on his driver and the other pressing a secure satellite phone against his ear. He scanned left and right as he listened to the President, shaking his head at the glut of security personnel posted along the course and around the private resort. The entire property had been shut down and reserved for the annual retreat of key Republican leaders in the U.S. House and Senate, which amounted to just over three hundred lawmakers and staffers. To Johnson, it seemed as if there were just as many security personnel.

Who knew we had so many "key leaders" in the party anyway?

"I hear that, Mr. President. Why can't we just make decisions in smoke-filled rooms like they do in the movies? It would be so much more ... efficient. Wouldn't you say, Sir?"

The President grunted his approval.

Johnson had supported and advised President Calhoun since he first burst onto the South Carolina political scene in one of the biggest upsets in U.S. House of Representatives history. Calhoun, a descendant of U.S. Vice President John C. Calhoun, was a latecomer to politics after making a name for himself as a state prosecutor where he focused on punishing corrupt politicians.

In his first campaign, he hadn't thrown his hat into the ring until the last minute before the primaries and still ended up winning the general election by more than fifteen points. Four years later, he fought hard to win a seat in the U.S. Senate. After he served two terms there, the people of South Carolina sent him to Columbia as governor, where he lived in the Executive Mansion—an historic structure that once housed faculty for South Carolina's institutional precursor to his alma mater, the Citadel.

"As a group, they certainly complain a lot. But I guess you can't really blame them, not after seeing what they have to endure from their constituencies these days. Everyone has someone to answer to, right?"

Johnson knew exactly what the President was getting at. Waving to the three junior senators in his foursome to go ahead and tee off, he walked a few paces from the tee box to get some privacy. "Yes, Mr. President. That is undoubtedly true."

"Well, the people we answer to are growing impatient about Judge Midas. Get him confirmed. Make whatever deals you need to—just get it done before you step down and become National Security Advisor. You've always come through for me, and this time I'm really counting on you."

"Mr. President, I have twisted every arm I can reach for over two hundred days. If there were some deal that could be struck, I would have found it by now. We may want to consider—"

The President cut him off. "No. There's nothing else to consider. There's still some time on the clock. You've never let me down before; I know you won't start now. I have to run. Before I go, tell me, what do you need from me?"

Johnson approached the golf cart, placed his driver in his bag, and tapped his bodyguard on the shoulder. "Move over," he whispered. Then he sat behind the wheel and leaned back. "If you want me to get this done—can you lend me the real launch codes? As opposed to the watered-down nuclear option I have at my disposal in the Senate."

The President thought for a moment before answering. "I don't think so. Best I can offer you is second-in-line, but we have some things to accomplish first. Are you meeting with Landry?"

"Yes, but I'm much more concerned with domestic political challenges and the future of our beloved republic at the moment than with yet another classified outfit to babysit."

"Hmmm. How about we merge the two then? How about a classified outfit you can also use to solve domestic political problems? That you don't have to babysit. Talk soon."

The line went dead. Johnson drove the cart forward and called out to the rest of his foursome. "I'm done, gents. Heading up to the big house. Finish without me."

The cart path ran parallel to the fairway for about two hundred yards before coming to a fork. Johnson turned right and headed up the hill to the clubhouse.

"Good morning, Senator Johnson. What can we do for you?" asked the hostess in the main dining room.

"All set for now, young lady. I have an urgent matter to attend to, but when I return, I'll have breakfast with my friend here." He pointed to the bodyguard. "Would you be so kind as to seat him somewhere to wait for me?"

Johnson waved and shook a few hands on his way to the narrow hallway at the far end of the room. He followed it to the end, opened the last door on the right, and entered a private locker room where all the furniture and lockers had been removed and a temporary sensitive compartmented information facility (SCIF) tent erected in their place. It filled half of the main room.

An aide unzipped the tent's opening and held up the flap for Johnson to enter. Then he closed it tightly and motioned to his colleague that the SCIF was secure. Inside, two chairs were facing each other. Senator Johnson sat in the empty one and reached down with one hand to grab a bottle of water from the floor. He twisted open the cap and drank half the bottle in one swig.

"Being the U.S. Senate majority leader from the great state of North Carolina, I normally have to choose my words very carefully. But since we're sitting in one of the most secure places on earth at the moment, I'm going to loosen up a little and share something with you." He screwed the cap back onto the water bottle and leaned forward. "I despise golf."

"Me too," answered Mark.

. . .

Senator Johnson listened as Mark summed up his assessment of the current threat from Islamic terrorists. The senator jotted down notes and questions on a piece of paper that would need to be shredded prior to leaving the SCIF.

"The bottom line is that as the so-called Caliphate loses ground, the foreign fighters won't be able to just take off their black pajamas and blend into the crowd. They'd stick out like sore thumbs. So they'll head back to their native countries. The so-called lone wolves are bad enough—although in most cases we find out after the fact that they were on some kind of watch list, so they're more like "known wolves" who just weren't stopped. Now imagine thousands of homegrown men and women who were willing to join an apocalyptic cult, coming back to their former countries with training and combat experience. For us, it's a bad dream. For Europe, it's a nightmare. Add to that the growing number of attacks in the U.S. where the terrorists use vehicles against pedestrians, and we still have plenty to worry about."

"And how would you advise using your team in that area?"

"I'd say use us to augment existing counterterror units when necessary. Pick up the slack when and where we can. But there are already enough dedicated CT assets and resources, so I wouldn't want that as our primary focus."

"Then what should your focus be?"

"Big picture? The rise of non-state actors over the past few decades has gotten countries to take their eyes off their main competition—other states. You're an historian, Senator. I'm not telling you anything you don't already know. States go down because they get distracted or caught up in infighting instead of paying attention to the rising powers on the periphery. When they finally wake up, it's too late. My team would serve at your pleasure, but if I had my choice I'd focus on state actors—North Korea, Iran, and Russia, to name a few. They play dirty pool because they get away with it. We need to send a clear message that those days are over."

"Goddamned Russians are popping up everywhere lately. A three-hundred-foot vessel packed with electronic surveillance equipment left Cuba a week ago and has been creeping its way up the east coast. It's parked off Cherry Point, North Carolina as we speak— which is like the Kremlin waving its dick in my face. Needless to say, I don't like it." Johnson looked at his watch. He only had a few minutes left before he needed to wrap things up and get back to the retreat. "Do you think there might be more to this recent incident up in Boston with the new guy at the Russian Embassy? What was his name, Borodin?"

"Oleg Borodin, and yes. FBI assets had been watching him closely since he arrived at the embassy two months ago. He played the role of the bean-counting bureaucrat as long as he could. Spent most of his days walking around the embassy, bothering people about expense reports and time cards. As soon as they backed off surveillance, he somehow ended up in Boston with a thug who tried to kill one of my guys—something I cannot tolerate. He showed up at Logan Airport less than an hour after shots were fired with nothing but the clothes on his back and a diplomatic passport. The whole time, he was making a show of how quickly he needed to get home to his dying mother—a story I'm sure the Russian government was prepared to corroborate, complete with a corpse and obituary, if pressed. But he touched down in Moscow just long enough to catch a flight to Prague. As far as I know, he's still there. I'm told he has a network of operatives and co-optees scattered across the U.S. We have a phone and some other data we're still trying to extract information from, but his identity and role in espionage have already been corroborated by a credible foreign intelligence service."

Keeping his eyes on Mark, Johnson pointed toward the tent ceiling above their heads with an index finger. "We're in an SCIF, Mark. And we don't keep secrets from each other, right?"

"German BND. Someone I've worked with before and know personally. Someone I can trust. She flew here specifically to share the information with me." Mark wondered if Johnson knew enough about the Berlin mission to connect the dots. The way the Majority Leader nodded and the quick flicker in his eyes indicated that he did.

"I agree that he needs to be held accountable. What do you suggest we do with him, Mark?"

"Anything but the usual. Too predictable. Typically, we round up a bunch of Russian diplomats and businesspeople, declare them persona non grata and write frustrated letters to places like the UN, where Russia can veto anything that comes before the Security Council anyway. Meanwhile the Russians are laughing at us the whole time and harassing American diplomats around the globe. They get followed everywhere. Their homes get broken into when they're out. Their kids get harassed at school. The Russians do it because they know the worst that'll happen to them is being declared persona non grata and sent back home. Which would be a badge of honor for them. But this guy Borodin is different. He crossed the Rubicon." Mark paused and looked around at the tent that enveloped the two men. Then he looked back at Senator Johnson and matter-of-factly added, "So we need to send a much different message than usual. Borodin obviously needs to die a very painful and horrible death. But first we must disrupt and destroy his networks in the U.S. and Europe. Hit them near and far—harder and faster than we ever have before, because it's the only thing they understand. They don't care about sanctions and diplomacy. It just gives them more time and space—the two things you want to deny your prey once you've closed in for the kill. We need to take the gloves off and attack quickly with overwhelming force. This is something we should have done when the Soviet Union collapsed. Instead, we let the KGB morph into a criminal-political partnership of thugs with nuclear weapons and no scruples. Now we're paying for it."

Johnson gave no reaction. He just pretended to be glancing down at his notepad. Mark could see he was distracted but continued.

"Tracking and eliminating Borodin should be priority. All our resources are focused on him right now."

"Okay. I appreciate you coming in again, Mark."

Seriously? That's it? Is he going to put this off again? Hasn't he made a decision yet? Are we standing the Family back up or not? Is he still considering going with another outfit? Or do I have to throw my Hail Mary pass now to close this deal?

Johnson sensed Mark's uneasiness and pressed him. "Unless there's something else we need to talk about?"

Fuck it. It's now or never.

"Yeah, there is. But only if Judge Midas's SCOTUS confirmation is still a priority for you and the President."

Johnson glanced up immediately from his notepad. "Come again?"

"I know how you can get that sixtieth vote for Judge Midas. You've spent six months trying to flip a moderate Democrat to no avail. None of them will budge. I have reliable intelligence on a less likely member who is dying for a big win and willing to make a deal to get it. I'm certain of it. That is, if you're interested."

. . .

Other than a few friendly nods to the resort staff, Mark kept his head down as he exited through the spacious marble lobby. Media access was tightly controlled, so the gaggles of staffers strewn about were more relaxed than usual. They were too busy relaxing to even notice an unfamiliar man as he weaved his way through the crowd.

Getting into his vehicle, he reflected on the guarantee he had just given to Senator Johnson.

No backing out now, Landry. You've made the promise. You're committed. Now you need to deliver.

CHAPTER EIGHT: Connecting the Dots

"You guys still don't have any idea who he was?" asked Patty.

"Nope. No idea." Kenny hated lying, but Dunbar and Mark had purposely built a culture at Imperium that kept all business to themselves unless sharing it was absolutely necessary. This is a good operational security practice in general, but it also served as reciprocity to the PMC Wall. Their position was that if government institutions were going to require special permission and paperwork every time Imperium needed access to a resource, they couldn't expect to simply pick up the phone and start asking Mark's team questions whenever they needed something. Besides, Kenny was looking to court Patty, not push her away with revelations about his checkered past. There would be plenty of opportunities to share more if things continued to get serious.

"Well, you've been looking better and better. And you sound upbeat—distracted but upbeat."

"Yeah, thanks," Kenny answered.

"Yeah, thanks? That's the best you can do? Look at me and think of something sweet to say. I'll wait," she said playfully while batting her eyes.

Kenny took a quick look around his workstation to make sure he was alone. Then he looked into the camera and spoke in a low voice. "I do feel better. And once things quiet down around here, I look forward to picking things up where we left off."

"Much better." She touched the tips of her fingers to her puckered lips and blew a kiss into the camera. Kenny closed his eyes and pretended to feel it landing right smack dab on his lips.

"Let's make that happen soon," he added.

"Kenny, I think I have something here," exclaimed the new guy, approaching his workstation.

Kenny said goodbye to Patty and turned his attention to the visitor.

"I gotta go, Patty. I'll give you a call later."

"What have you got?" Kenny asked the new guy. "Wait, let's go to where you guys are working. I need to stretch my legs anyway."

Two other cyber-operators were hunkered down in front of a monitor. Both had been with Imperium for several years, yet neither had any problem with the new guy doing the talking. Less time talking meant more time could be spent doing what they did best—looking at complex programming code and analyzing global Internet traffic. They both looked up and nodded at Kenny. Then the new guy started briefing him on their progress.

"First, the Venezuelan passport that the deceased had in his possession when he attacked you has never been used. But that's not a surprise, because it was issued on the same day. We can't determine which consulate it was officially issued out of, but we do know that it was put into the Venezuelan national passport control system that same morning."

"Okay. Not bad. Useful information. What else have you got?"

"It gets better. We can't crack the phone through brute force, but we just got lucky with a side-channel attack. I think it was a flashlight app with some little known vulnerabilities we were able to exploit. We can't see everything on the phone, but we were able to retrieve all of its GPS location data. The phone was activated in Washington that morning. Then it traveled right up to Boston. Along the way he gassed up once. The only other stops were in Providence, Rhode Island."

"Where did they stop in Providence?" Kenny asked.

"The first stop was at an office supply store where they spent like fifteen minutes. After that, they stopped briefly at a gas station. That's all we got from the phone."

"What about the files we got from the German BND? Some of the files were open and some were encrypted. What were the open files, and can we read any of the encrypted files yet?"

"There's an executive summary from German intelligence on this Oleg Borodin guy. The Germans believe he manages global networks of spies, informants, hackers, and thugs for the FSB out of Anapa, Russia. They believe a treasure trove of information regarding Russian networks inside the United States are within the encrypted files that they have been unable to break. We're not having much more luck. The ones we can read just have names and addresses, but there's gotta be over ten thousand of them. We're trying to figure out what—if anything—ties them all together. Keeping in mind that we're dealing with Russians and how much they love disinformation, it could just be random chunks of phone books thrown together for no reason at all. We'll keep working on the encrypted files."

"Yeah. Well, maybe one day we'll have a master key, but for now we have to grind it out like this. Good work. Send the cell phone GPS history to my workstation, will you? As well as whatever is readable from the German data. Then I need all three of you to come over and wait while I figure out what's next. Thanks."

Kenny returned to his desk and pulled his big padded headphones over his ears. He scrolled through his music albums, selected "Monster Hits of the 80s," and hit *play*. Billy Idol's "Dancin' with Myself" started bouncing around between his ears as he got to work.

This would be a hell of a lot easier with the right permissions. But hey, you gotta do what you gotta do, right?

The first thing he did was to drill down to the two locations where the Russian pair had stopped on their way to Boston: the office supply store and the gas station. Once he had determined the exact locations he spun around and pointed to the first person he saw. "You," he said way too loud due to Billy Idol blaring in his ears. "Get the security footage from the office supply store and the gas station. Thank you."

Kenny spun back around and scrolled through the troves of names in the German data in silence for three or four minutes. There were a ridiculous number of names in the files, and he had no idea what, if anything, they would be able to get from the encrypted files. Kenny turned around and pointed to the next guy. "You can start with these lists. Do whatever you have to do to determine if any of these people are located anywhere near Providence. Got it?" Kenny shouted. His coworker nodded and left. Kenny put the headphones on top of his head and turned to address the new guy who had been doing the talking. He still had to talk loudly to be heard over the music.

"You can get back to your station and start packing your stuff."

"What? Pack my stuff for what?" he asked anxiously. It sounded to him like an unceremonious firing. But why?

"Because I'm impressed and I want you working close to me from now on. Unless you'd rather not."

"Of course I do. Thanks for the opportunity. Could I just make one request, though? You keep calling me new guy. I know I've only been here for a few months, but my name is—"

"I know what your name is, Robby. Just go get your stuff so we can get to work, okay?"

"Actually, it's Robert."

"Go before I change my mind!"

Kenny dropped the headphones back over his ears and sat down in front of his tri-monitor display. He tapped his hands along with the music on the desktop and focused his mind on the question at hand.

Where did Dmitri get a Venezuelan passport? Start by locating all Venezuelan state assets along his route of travel that day. Add prominent Venezuelan businesspeople to the mix. Known criminals wouldn't hurt. Search the Dark Web for current chatter on best fake IDs. Who are the top fake ID producers in the area? Start with them. Are any of them Venezuelan? Can we squeeze anyone in the Venezuelan government to find out where the passport was issued? Do they even know? Lots of questions and very few answers. So turn up the music and get cracking, Kenny.

CHAPTER NINE: The Offer

"Well, thank God for strong women like you, Lois. What was it that Abigail Adams once wrote about men? That if left unsupervised they would all be dictators? Something like that, right?" asked Georgina Johnson.

"Close. 'Remember, all men would be tyrants if they could,' " McDermott quoted verbatim.

"It was true then and it is truer today, so I will say it again. Thank God for strong women like you, Lois. Tough women. Visionary women who can see the big picture. Isn't that right, sweetheart?" Georgina asked her husband with a smile.

Senator Johnson smiled awkwardly at his wife and reached for his glass.

Pouring it on a little thick, aren't you, Ginny? You know that Abigail Adams quote darn well. And you know it's displayed on McDermott's office wall. And she knows that you know. I said McDermott was malleable. But she is certainly not stupid.

"It's good to see you two are having so much fun this evening. Like two peas in a pod, I must say," he replied.

More like two halves of a vise with my nuts in the middle. I got more irons in the fire right now than a horse has hair. Can we please get on with the evening?

He sipped his drink and checked the grandfather clock against the far wall of the dining room. It was getting near time to wrap up and move on to the main event in his private study.

Georgina took her cue. She reached across the dining room table and put a hand on one of McDermott's. "Well, I know you two probably have some sort of business to discuss, so I'll take my leave and let you relocate to the study where you can talk. That's always been our agreement," she said, looking adoringly at her laconic husband. "No politics at the table. Save it for later because dinner time is family time, and family is the only thing that matters. And God bless my husband because he has never broken that rule, and I think that is one of the things that has kept us happily together for more than forty years."

Give it a break, Ginny. We never talk about anything but politics. And you know exactly what we're about to talk about in the study.

Johnson dabbed at the corner of his mouth with his napkin, then placed it on the table next to his plate. "Yes, ma'am. That is very true. And I'm sure Senator McDermott will keep that in mind should she ever decide to settle down again." He regretted that remark as soon as he said it and quickly pivoted. "Perhaps you'd like to use the restroom first, Lois. Afterwards, my study is down the hall, last room on the left."

"On the left, eh? And you still bought the place?" McDermott answered.

. . .

McDermott swirled her glass a few times. Then she took another small sip and held the glass to her nose again. "Never had it before. But I gotta say it's living up to the hype."

Johnson took a long sip and let the elixir roll off and under his tongue. "It's the one thing we can always be certain of—Johnnie Walker Black is the best blended scotch in the history of the world."

"Well, so far we're in agreement. Should we stop here, or is there something else you wanted to talk to me about?"

"Midas."

"The judge or the muffler shop?"

"The judge," Johnson answered. "Obviously."

"I think we've already talked about him. Unless you're referring to a different Midas."

"I'm not. And I'm not interested in talking about him anymore either. I have only one question for you."

"What's your question?"

"What would it take? What would it take to get your vote for his confirmation?"

McDermott was taken aback at the assumption that there was any way she would support Judge James Midas's confirmation.

"Nothing. It's not possible. Honestly, the president should have withdrawn his nomination long ago and offered a more suitable, more mainstream candidate for the court. It's that simple." She took another sip of the Johnnie Walker Black. "This is good, but it ain't that good."

"What about this?" Johnson placed his drink on the coffee table between them and walked behind his oak desk. He tapped a few keys on his computer and turned his monitor around so that McDermott could see the image. It was an old photo taken inside a passenger plane.

"What's that? An empty plane?"

"Look closer."

McDermott squinted and leaned toward Johnson's desk to get a better look. "Are those baby cribs strapped into the seats?"

"Yes they are. Operation Babylift. Vietnam, 1975. By the time the operation was over, the U.S. had rescued over ten thousand orphans and placed them in American families willing and able to adopt. It was the right thing to do. And it was good PR for the country. If we can do the right thing for some of those refugee children you've been so concerned about and boost the American brand at the same time, well, that's something I think we can make happen."

McDermott picked up her glass from the table and sat back in her chair. Then she took a deep breath and a long sip before speaking. "I've been talking about those kids for almost two years and nobody on your side of the aisle, including you, would even talk with me about it."

"We're talking about it now. Isn't that what you wanted? Besides, we're talking about a lot of kids, Lois."

"How many?"

Johnson smiled proudly, leaned back against his desk, and casually crossed his feet at the ankles. "Five thousand a year for five years. That's twenty-five thousand kids. More than twice the total of Operation Babylift."

She stood, walked closer to the screen with her glass in hand, and looked at the extraordinary photo. Then she narrowed her eyes and looked at Johnson. "But only if I vote to confirm a positively contemptible candidate for the highest court?"

Johnson rolled his eyes and waved both of his arms as if shooing flies. "Whatever, Lois. We are not here to clutch pearls. We're here to talk about the deal of the century—not just for you, but for a whole bunch of kids who aren't exactly getting much help lately. But I don't have a magic wand, so I'm telling you exactly what I need to make that happen."

"You're asking for too much, Senator. This isn't some small earmark in the annual budget. It's a lifetime appointment. And honestly, I'm a bit insulted."

Johnson picked up his glass and walked slowly to the opposite end of the room as he spoke. "I'm offering you something you've always wanted: quantifiable proof that you made a difference. I've been in the Senate for decades. Trust me, opportunities like this are once-in-a-lifetime. Besides, we all know that at the end of the day all politics is either a bribe or extortion, right? And I can't help but notice you're still in the room. So should I keep talking or not?"

McDermott was still shocked by the offer that had come out of left field, but after a few deep breaths she sat back down. Then she leaned forward and poured herself another glass of Johnnie Walker Black from Johnson's bottle.

"I'm listening."

· · ·

Mark's phone vibrated in his pocket and he checked his watch. *Right on time.*
MCDERMOTT: Are you in town?

He waited ten minutes, then texted back.

MARK: Yes, heading back to Boston. Will stop by on way to airport. Everything okay?
MCDERMOTT: Everything fine. Just wanted to talk.
MARK: I have time. Gimme 30 min.

Forty-five minutes later, Mark was sitting comfortably in the Senator's family room, watching her pace the floor and recount the details of her after-dinner meeting with Senator Johnson. She was obviously fired up about Johnson's offer—which meant that she was at least considering it. Why else would she have invited him over to discuss it?

"Wow. And was there was nobody else in the room?" he asked, acting surprised.

"Just us. And he was more serious than I have ever seen him. It was a little creepy but I kept it together."

"Was he hammered or something?"

"Stone cold sober. Are you going to miss your flight, Mark?"

"No. So what are you going to do about Johnson?"

"Are you sure? What time does it take off?"

"Later. Don't worry about it. Tell me more about Johnson. What are you going to do?"

McDermott stopped pacing and looked at Mark with a surprised expression on her anxious face. "Nothing. I could never vote for Midas. He's unfit. And part of me is insulted that he thought I could be bought off."

Mark nodded his head in agreement, but on the inside he was groaning in disbelief.

Really? Playing the integrity card now? What about the whopper of a lie you've been telling me?

"So what was it? Five thousand a year for five years? Twenty-five thousand kids saved? That sounds like a lot to me."

"A drop in the bucket. That wouldn't even put a dent in the orphan refugee crisis."

"So what?"

"So what? What do you mean, so what?"

"Maybe it doesn't solve the crisis, but it sure as hell would make a difference to those twenty-five thousand kids. At least they'd be saved. Let's not act like that's nothing."

"So you think I should vote to confirm Midas?" she asked.

"I didn't say that. I'm just saying that twenty-five thousand kids is a shitload of kids, right?"

"I'm not sure I'd use the same word choice, but—yes, it's a lot of kids."

"Something to consider."

"Can't." She sat down on the sofa next to Mark. "In exchange, I'd be putting a man on the court who could cause irreparable damage to our own citizens and the republic itself. The political consequences would be devastating. I'm talking about lights-out for America."

"Oh, please. I told you before I don't think it would be the end of the world if Midas were confirmed to the court. And even if he was as dangerous as you think, there are eight other justices perfectly capable of stopping a runaway colleague. So I don't understand how you're getting all the way to lights-out for America because of this one guy."

McDermott looked at her watch again and remembered that it was almost time to take her medicine. Her doctors had been adamant about not missing doses. "I thought you were on your way to the airport. Are you going to miss your flight?"

"No. Don't worry about it."

"Seriously, I'm wasting your time and talking your ear off. Go now if you have to."

"I said don't worry about it. How can Johnson be so certain he can even get this done? What did he say about families and funding and all that?"

"He said there are almost two million families right here in the United States who want to adopt. They've already applied and been vetted. The only things missing are babies. Demand is evidently much higher than the supply. The most expensive part of the program will be transporting the kids here. In reality, the rest of the work is already done. In fact, he's making it sound so easy that I'm wondering why we haven't already done something like it."

"Are there really that many people waiting?"

"Yeah, he's telling the truth. He also correctly pointed out that Russia no longer permits Americans to adopt Russian orphans. But he kept mentioning how good this would be for the American brand—as if the country were some kind of an athletic shoe or something."

Mark went to the kitchen and stood in front of the refrigerator. Then he opened both doors and started poking around inside. "Jeez, isn't there anything to eat in this house? Haven't you had time to go grocery shopping lately? I'm starving."

McDermott cocked her head sideways and watched him from the sofa. Mark kicked off his shoes and threw them across the room so that they landed next to the front door—the kind of thing people do only in their own home. She welcomed his newfound familiarity. It was a good sign. But it was all happening so fast as to be quite confusing, especially so late in the day when she was due for her medications.

Is our relationship warming this quickly? It's like he suddenly turned into a son at the flick of a switch.

"What's that, Mark?" She walked into the kitchen and stood behind her son.

"Nothing." He closed the refrigerator doors and turned around to face his mother. "But he's put you in one hell of a position, hasn't he?"

"Who? Johnson? Why would you say that? He's offering me the deal. I hold all the cards."

"No, you don't. He's made you an offer you can't refuse."

"How do you figure?"

"If you vote to confirm Midas, you save twenty-five thousand kids. If you don't, you'll obsess for the rest of your life about the twenty-five thousand kids you could have saved but didn't. He's got you right where he wants you. He holds all the cards."

McDermott thought about it. When it appeared that she was about to reply, Mark returned to the family room and sat on the sofa. She followed behind.

"That's one way to look at it, yes. But you're completely omitting the principle involved in the decision. Midas would be bad for America. I truly believe that. If I take this deal, I'm saying I can be bought. And I can't be bought. Don't forget about your flight, Mark."

Mark leaned back and clasped his hands behind his head. "Then tell him to pound sand."

"Tell Johnson to pound sand? Now you're saying not to take the deal?"

"I haven't advised you either way. I'm just pointing out things you might have missed. And I don't think your integrity is on the line. I'm not sure this is going to make you feel any better, but public opinion of Congress is pretty low to begin with. And nobody who matters would hold it against you once they saw a bunch of babies being rescued. Hell no, they'll wrap you in the flag and carry you around."

"Not everyone, Mark. There are a lot of people who would see it as a betrayal. And they would never forgive me. Some of them would make it their life's mission to make me miserable. There will be new death threats to add to my stack of existing death threats."

"Those who mind don't matter, and those who matter don't mind. And look, you already said you're leaning against running for reelection, right?"

"Not leaning against it. I'm not running. And isn't that a Doctor Seuss quote?"

"Really? That's Doctor Seuss? I thought Carlos and Amanda made it up. Anyway, if you're not running for reelection, what could the haters do to you then? Say mean things about you? Who cares? They do that already. You would have saved twenty-five thousand kids. And what would it look like if news of the offer leaked to the press after you turned it down? Would you be able to stand up there and say you consciously chose not to save that many orphans, all because James Midas is an asshole? The party diehards might applaud you, but nobody else on earth would understand how you turned your back on twenty-five thousand kids. Actually, I think you could get that number up pretty easily."

"How?"

"Johnson is the Senate Majority Leader, and everyone knows he's the president's bestie. He's also a dealmaker. Which means he probably came at you low. I bet you could go back at him and double that number. In fact, I bet he's ready for it."

"Really?" McDermott paced to the sliding glass door to her balcony—the same door that Mark casually strode through five years earlier. Now he was sitting in her living room having a serious conversation and slowly changing her mind on something monumental. She found the whole thing surreal.

"That's what I'd do. I'd tell him to double the number and he's got a deal. Fifty thousand kids. It's a no-brainer. I could give you some more pointers if you're interested."

Maybe he's right. But this is a lot to process. I should go and take my meds before I forget.

"I bet Megan would be back at your side in a flash if she had a chance to shape policy like that. Hell, Luci's been waiting for the right opportunity to come along. I can't speak for her, but I imagine she'd jump at the chance to help if you were working on something like this. I think the twins even did some kind of project related to the crisis in school. They sent care packages to refugee kids or something like that. I can't tell you how the rest of the world would react—you would know better than I—but at least you know the family would support you."

The family? Did he just call all of us a family? Or was it simply a slip of the tongue? Call him on it before you lose too much energy.

"Are you ready to meet Megan, Mark? I mean, really meet her? The longer I wait to tell her about you, the harder it's going to be for her to accept it. Especially after all we've been through together."

The question took Mark by surprise.

Wow. Had that ready to go, didn't you? Threw in the reminder about your losses as a kicker—something I have NEVER seen you do.

McDermott knew what was coming, so she quickly sat down on her favorite reading chair. If she didn't, she might get dizzy enough to fall. That had already happened once and she was petrified of it happening again—especially in front of Mark. Soon she was sitting and staring blankly in his direction.

Is she okay?

"Are you okay?"

No response.

"Hello? Are you okay?"

He stood up and walked slowly toward her chair. "Senator? Hello? Lois?" He waved a hand in front of her face.

No response.

This is a lot to handle, but she doesn't look well. Get her attention. You need her. Snap her out of it!

"Mom!" Mark yelled out.

McDermott shook off the fog and refocused on him.

What did he just call me?

"Yes, I'm sorry. I just drifted off for a minute. What were you saying? Do you have to go catch your flight?"

"No," Mark sighed as he knelt down beside her chair. "And for the last time, stop worrying about my flight. It won't leave without me. It's Imperium's plane and I'm the only passenger."

"One day you're going to have to tell me more about exactly what this company of yours does. In the meantime, you mentioned that you had some other pointers on how to make the deal even better."

She reached over and grasped Mark's hand.

"I'm listening, Son. What do you think I should do?"

CHAPTER TEN: Decrypted

Billy slid a chair next to Kenny's workstation and sat down. He pulled the Oklahoma cap from his head and tossed it onto the desk. Then he leaned back, crossed his legs, and popped open his second twenty-ounce Red Bull of the night. "Tell me what you've got."

"Right now, Robby is checking the list of rotating IP addresses we got from the hard drive in the copy machine at the office supply store," Kenny answered without looking up.

"Good. Now explain to me exactly what the hell all that is supposed to mean. I have time."

"Right. Sorry, Billy. Here's where we are right now." Kenny sent his files to the big screen on the wall behind his desk.

Kenny pulled up the video of the two Russian men from the gas station first. Borodin stayed in the car while Dmitri pumped gas. When he finished, he went inside the store and paid cash. Then he exited and started to drive away. Just when the car was about to leave camera range, it came to a stop. A tall white male wearing a blue hoodie approached the open passenger side window and gesticulated as if giving directions. During the exchange, he dropped a small brown envelope into Borodin's lap. Kenny and Robby had to watch the video several times before catching the drop.

"Pretty sloppy tradecraft to be doing anything important right there, isn't it?" noted Billy. "I guess that's what happens when you merge professional Russian intelligence operatives and common thugs into one big happy family. It comes with a cost."

"It does," Kenny answered. "Dmitri was never the sharpest pencil in the box in the first place. And from what I remember, he was hammered more often than not. Never a clear thinker. Maybe that's why he started beating on me when he recognized me in Boston instead of just killing me. His sloppiness bought me time and eventually my life. Thanks to you, Billy. That's the second time you've saved my hide. The first was getting me out of jail and delivering me to Doc. Then you stopped a crazy Russian from killing me in front of my girlfriend."

"No worries. Glad to have been in a position to do so. Wish I could have gotten to this guy before he got his hands on you."

Kenny returned his attention to the screen. He didn't want to talk anymore about Billy saving his ass again. He felt bad enough. He alone was responsible for the incident. He had brought trouble into the Imperium house and caused problems for everyone. He had made the mess. Now he wanted to be damn sure he got the chance to clean it up and redeem himself. He kept his composure and continued briefing Billy.

"So here's where we got even luckier. The guy who dropped the envelope into their car is no genius either. Ten minutes after Dmitri and Borodin drove away, he bought a can of soda and a candy bar at the same gas station. He could have gone anywhere in Providence, but he decided to go right back to where he had just met his contacts. Which means he's not very bright or simply not worried about getting caught. Here he is entering the store through the main door. That's him. Same clothes. Everything. We couldn't have asked for a better shot."

Kenny showed a clear full-color photo of the unknown male entering the gas station. He was tall, thin, and unshaven. Shaggy black hair with matching scruff. Dressed in a hoodie and sweatpants.

"We've sent the image out to all the usual agencies. Hopefully facial recognition will kick up something useful. It could take a while, and you never know. But things get even better with the next video. Watch this."

Kenny cued up the video from the office supply store.

"Dmitri and Oleg Borodin both enter. Borodin speaks to an

employee, who points to the back of the store. Borodin grabs a magazine from the rack on his way back toward the bathroom. Dmitri waits a few minutes before going over to a photocopy machine. He takes out the envelope they just got from the drop—"

Billy cut him off. "How do we know for sure that it's the same envelope?"

"Watch Dmitri," Kenny said, pointing to the monitor as he zoomed in on the Russian. "Look closely. He made two copies. One of his new Venezuelan passport and one of a handwritten note that was inside the passport. He scribbled something on it just before making the copy."

"Why would he do that? Why make extra copies?"

"No idea. The guy was a drunken idiot, so I don't waste much time trying to rationalize his actions. Should I continue? There's more."

"Please do."

"The passport we already have, but we obviously wanted to know what the other piece of paper had on it. Thankfully, the copy machines and print shop are all connected to the company's servers, so we were able to get into the copy machine."

"Okay. What good does that do?"

"Quite a bit. By definition, a photocopier takes a picture of the original document and then copies it onto a piece of paper. To do so, it needs a way to remember the image. Most machines use small drives of flash memory to make that happen. As a side effect, the image remains there in the copier's limited memory until it gets forced out by newer images from new copies."

"So that's how you got the note? That's brilliant. Very cutting-edge of you."

"Not really. It's actually kind of old-school, like checking typewriter ribbons for clues in old detective stories. Just a more updated version."

"So what was the note about?"

"Scribbled numbers that appear to be dates, times, and IP addresses. No words at all except for what Dmitri wrote at the bottom:

'MendaxIsDead.' No idea what that means, but we've pinpointed the exact locations of the IP addresses and they are all in or around Providence. Robby is speaking to NSA about getting traffic reports from those addresses on the specific dates and times mentioned. We want to know who they connected with online and where during those windows. Hopefully, there's a pattern that will tell us more."

"Good work, Kenny. I'm impressed."

"We haven't accomplished anything yet." Kenny's desk phone beeped twice and flashed Robby's name. He reached over and put the call on speakerphone. "Tell me something good, Robby."

"Yeah. Quick question on the traffic history on those IP addresses you asked me to get. Are you a level 3 or above supervisor with prior authorization? And does this pertain to an active investigation in which a FISA warrant has been issued?"

Kenny rolled his eyes. Obviously, in his quest to fulfill Kenny's orders, Robby had been asked those questions by the NSA or a similar outfit. He had not been around long enough to know how to handle this type of situation. Kenny had. The culture created at Imperium by Dunbar and Mark was clear—ask for permission as rarely as possible and keep all cards close to the vest.

Kenny looked at Billy. "Looks like I'm going to have to take care of this myself. The new guy doesn't know the right things to say to get what he wants yet. I'll let you know what turns up." Billy grabbed his cap from the desk and waved goodbye as he walked away. Then Kenny picked up the handset and spoke to Robby. "Go ahead and just transfer them to me. I'll take it from here and let you know what turns up."

"Okay. We also just got a possible facial recognition match for the guy who made the drop. It looks like a match to me. Should I send that over too?"

"Yes, transfer the NSA call to me and send the facial recognition match immediately. Then stand by. I'm sure it won't be long before I need you for something."

...

Kenny spent the next forty-five minutes being transferred between the same four people inside NSA and other private contractors before finally convincing them to authorize his request for information.

It's all about hitting the right buttons. Saying the right things. Making it crystal clear that their own sorry asses are covered. That's when they usually open right up.

"Okay, thanks. I'll be looking for that in the next few minutes, then. Thank you very much." Kenny pulled up the information on the potential facial recognition match and sat back in his chair. Then he gulped the final bit of cold coffee in his mug, put on his glasses, and squinted at the image on the screen. The photo was a little grainy, but he could still see the hoodied figure's face well enough to perceive the likeness. The picture appeared to have been snapped at an ATM.

That looks like him all right. What's his story?

The information attached to the photo had been disseminated to FBI field offices several months ago. A person of interest related to international cyber crimes. Real name unknown. Kenny skimmed the rest of the information until something jumped out at him. On a list of suspected screen names appeared the name MendaxIsDead. He remembered that Dmitri had scribbled the same thing on the bottom of the photocopied note. Then came more information on suspected crimes. Kenny cringed as he read about the suspect's involvement with the creation of an online pedophile exchange known as Playpen that the FBI had taken down in a sophisticated cyber sting. The other jobs to which he was connected were not your run-of-the-mill criminal activity. Men willing to do routine stuff are a dime a dozen. This guy was different. MendaxIsDead was a freelance hacker with no conscience. He did jobs and facilitated financial transactions for organizations involved in child trafficking, weapons smuggling, narco-trafficking, and snuff movies. Material support to Islamic terror cells. Zero scruples. The kind of guy who wouldn't think twice about helping Russian agents.

The connection history for the IP addresses listed in the note arrived in Kenny's mailbox. He clicked on the secure file from NSA.

His system decrypted and opened it. Kenny made the image as big as he could and sat back with folded arms. For the next several minutes, his eyes darted up and down, left and right as he absorbed and processed the information.

The IP addresses were from specific locations, mostly around Providence, with one just over the border into Connecticut. He kept reading and looked at the traffic reports for the specific dates and times mentioned in the note.

Bingo. At the specific dates and times, someone, more than likely this dirtbag MendaxIsDead, established secure connections with the same server out of Anapa, Russia. Each time, a whole bunch of encrypted files were transferred back and forth. German intel says Borodin is managing networks of spies and operatives within the country. Could this be how they've been receiving instructions? Is this one of the ways they communicate?

Kenny looked more closely at the dates on the note. There were ten in all. He was looking at the available data on the first eight. The other two dates had not yet passed. He glanced at the *Lord of the Rings* calendar taped to the side of his workstation.

Shit. The next one is in a few hours. The final date is next week.

He stroked a few keys on his computer and checked on the location indicated for later that evening. A strip club in a dive area of Providence. Something about a DJ booth mentioned in the original installation data. Kenny looked around at the rest of his coworkers still trying to hack their way into Dmitri's burner phone and weighed his options.

Why not let them continue with the brute force approach while I see if I can intercept the data transmission? If I pull it off, I'll be back with the latest communication between Russia and its networks and a decryption key that may very well work on the burner phone too. This may be the one opportunity I ever get to prove myself. If I get there and don't think I can pull it off, I can always walk away and tell Mark. According to the note, there will be one more data transfer date next week. But if I want to redeem myself and prove that I don't need to be babysat or saved—to prove I'm a man—this may be the only opportunity I ever get.

Kenny knew the new operator, David, might be a problem.

Since the incident with Dmitri, he had been shadowing Kenny and even sleeping on the sofa in his apartment as a security precaution. Mark wouldn't let him stand down yet and Kenny knew it would cause suspicion if he started to complain about it now.

Kenny called David to let him know he would be leaving in a few minutes. He was tired and wanted to rest for a few hours before coming back.

"No problem, I'll meet you down in the parking garage."

The pair small-talked about Boston sports on the way to Kenny's second-story Back Bay apartment. Kenny was cheerful and David was glad that his new coworker had not resisted his constant presence as much as Mark had expected him to do. Kenny was all right. And things were going quite smoothly.

Kenny held up his cellphone on the way to his bedroom. "I'll have this with me, but I need to turn it off for a few hours so I can catch some Z's. Don't wake me up unless the building is on fire."

"Will do. I'll be snoozing out here on the couch if you need me."

"I won't." Kenny closed his bedroom door and locked it.

He sent a goodnight text to Patty.

Fifteen minutes later, Kenny stuffed his car keys into his pocket and tied a black and grey flannel scarf around his head to cover his face, leaving only a tiny slit open for his eyes. Then he climbed out his bedroom window and stepped onto the fire escape.

. . .

Kenny had correctly estimated the distance from the fire escape to the top of the dumpster, but he had not anticipated the smooth layer of ice hiding under a thick, white blanket of fresh powder. The balls of his feet made contact with the slippery surface first; his tailbone and the back of his head followed a split second thereafter.

He bounced and found himself airborne again before landing on the much less forgiving pavement with a muted thud, his right knee absorbing much of the impact. He immediately rolled to his back and pulled his knee into his chest with both hands. With two feet of snow on the ground—and counting—it was unlikely that anyone would have been outside to see him. But sound travels faster and farther on windless, snowy nights. He stifled the impulse to scream out in pain.

Kenny lay still and breathed deeply for several minutes, hoping that David had not heard the commotion, before slowly getting to his feet and dusting off his snow-covered body. He stuffed his hands into the front pockets of his navy blue pea coat to readjust the Smith and Wesson Bodyguard .380 and spare magazines, and to make sure that his secure phone and other items had not tumbled out.

He located his car keys and pulled the thick wool hat down tight around his ears. Then he limped to the end of the alley and turned right onto the main road to find his car.

In spite of the snow, the ride to Providence went much quicker than expected. There were few cars on the road, and most of the trip was down I-95 behind a line of emergency snow plows. He parked several blocks from the strip club in an out-of-the-way lot next to an abandoned warehouse. Then he headed for the main intersection. ...

In the strip club was Kenny's final destination: a thick, plexiglass-encased DJ booth. A tall, thin man wearing a hoodie and matching the pictures of MendaxIsDead was working inside the booth, ready to establish a secure connection with the Russian FSB. No idea he was about to be killed by another hacker, known as the Hobbit.

Kenny raised his weapon and aligned his sights on the back of the DJ's hoodie-covered head. Then he adjusted his two-handed grip on the compact .380, bent his knees, and took a deep breath. When MendaxIsDead turned around and charged with a humongous knife in his hands, Kenny pulled the trigger twice. ...

Kenny used the tip of the knife to dislodge the frozen computer chip from its position in MendaxIsDead's computer. Then he quickly snapped it into place in his own handheld machine and waited to see if it could read the data.

Come on ... come on ... come on! Read it! Read it!

The screen turned blue, confirming that the chip was readable.

Kenny initiated the process to copy all readable files and slipped the handheld machine back into the deep pocket of his pea coat. Then he stuffed the DJ's laptop and personal belongings into a nearby backpack, verified the status of his weapon, and walked out of the club with the bag slung over his shoulder.

Once back in the car, he initiated an encrypted connection with the Imperium's secure servers while ignoring the vibrating phone in his right cargo pocket as long as he could. He had been masking his location since slipping out of his apartment. Finally, he pulled it out and answered without looking at it. He didn't have to look. The same person—Mark Landry—had been calling for the past two hours.

"Go ahead, Mark."

Mark exhaled and paused for a second before speaking. He was clearly pissed.

"Kenny, where the hell are you?"

"I just turned off my masking app. My location should be popping back onto the grid right now. Mark, I know you're mad, but I intercepted a transmission between the Russians and their domestic agents and I have the decryption code we need to read it. I already started uploading info to Imperium's servers and I'm on my way back right now."

Kenny quickly apologized for slipping out his apartment window and recounted his trek to the strip club for Mark. The DJ booth. MendaxIsDead coming at him with a knife. Firing two shots into the hacker's head. Using a can of compressed air to freeze the system's memory chips and preserve the decryption code.

Mark was only somewhat surprised to hear about Kenny's solo quest for the decryption key. Since Kenny's recent revelation about his involvement with Russian organized crime figures, Mark figured there was still a lot to learn about his colleague and former neighbor anyway. Besides, compared to a trip to Russia to steal money from mobsters, running out in the middle of the night to pop one unsuspecting hacker didn't seem like that big of a deal—although Mark realized that this was almost certainly Kenny's first killing.

Mark sent a team to meet Kenny halfway between Boston and Providence. When the two vehicles linked up, two operators stayed with Kenny while the other two raced south to the strip club to take care of MendaxIsDead's body. Mark wanted the Russians to think their guy was alive for as long as possible. Hopefully nobody had seen his carcass and sounded the alarm.

When Kenny and his operator escorts walked into the Imperium Game Room in Boston, all cyber hands were on deck waiting to dive into the new data.

Kenny knew his decision to fly solo would be controversial, but he was proud of what he had done. He had been the root of the problem in the first place. His past had put people he cared about in danger. The past that he had been unable to completely shake had come back to bite not just him in the ass, but the colleagues and team members who had become his family. And now he had fixed it. On his own. Like a man.

. . .

It was just after 4:00 a.m. when Senator Johnson's personal cellphone started vibrating on his nightstand. He reached for his glasses first. Then he glanced at the alarm clock and answered the phone as he sat up and felt around for his bedroom slippers so he could move to the office. Anyone with this particular number had it for a reason.

"Wait."

Mark imagined Johnson wrapping himself in a plush robe and shuffling slowly down a long hall so they could speak privately.

"Okay. Go ahead. What have you got?"

"Two things, sir."

First, Mark reported that Imperium had just uncovered proof of Oleg Borodin's covert network operating within the U.S.

"Define proof for me, Mark. What exactly have you got? How comprehensive is it all?"

"The amount and depth of the disinformation, disruption, and deception campaigns are staggering. It's a treasure trove of information. Analysts are still poring through it all, but one thing is clear—Russian operatives are scattered across the country. They are embedded in the media, business groups, local and state governments, militias, right- and left-wing extremist groups—you name it. There's hundreds of pages of data, including very specific instructions for each group telling them exactly what to do to create as much chaos as possible."

"How do you know it is all legit?" It was Johnson's job to be skeptical and measured. That's how he got to be Senate Majority Leader and why he would soon become National Security Advisor.

"We don't. It's still new and there are still a lot of unanswered questions. Hundreds of names to verify and vet. However, the information so far seems to corroborate what our German friends have been saying. Winter isn't coming; apparently, it's already here. We'll need to hit them hard and fast in the U.S. first. Then hit them even harder in Europe."

Johnson went silent for a moment while he considered the news. Both men were frustrated that American officials hadn't unmasked Borodin's network sooner, but both knew better than to start assigning blame. There were simply too many potential bad guys and not enough agents and cops to surveille every one of them.

The senator exhaled and wondered what other great news Mark had for him so early in the morning. "Understood. You said you had two things for me. What's the other one?"

"I have intel on your SCOTUS confirmation."

Johnson sat back in the soft leather chair behind the large oak desk in his office and looked down at his slippers. Although Mark Landry had offered him few details as to how and why he knew that a particular U.S. Senator's vote could be bought, the McDermott deal had been worth the shot. But since the political fallout for confirming Judge Midas would be overwhelming for someone with her liberal bonafides, Johnson had little faith that she would take the deal.

It was a wild swing of the bat that he normally would have dismissed, but since Mark Landry had been anointed by Dunbar and the president had mentioned his respect for both Dunbar and Landry, Johnson had felt compelled to hear him out and give it a shot. Besides, solving the SCOTUS nomination was his number-one priority. If he couldn't get that done ASAP, then his and the president's long-term plans for the country would never come to fruition. Everything they wanted hinged on getting Midas confirmed.

Until now, Johnson still hadn't been sold on the idea of reforming the Family. That was about to change.

"What's your intel say, Mr. Landry? You think you can have that one wrapped up by noon today?" he asked sarcastically.

"Much earlier, actually. McDermott will be in your office in just a few hours to seal the deal."

. . .

McDermott knew Johnson was an early riser, so she went to his office first thing in the morning, hoping to get on the top of the list of people needing to speak with him that day. She pointed to the phone on the bubbly young receptionist's desk. "Go ahead. Give him a call to see what time he can squeeze me in today. I'll wait right here if you don't mind."

"Actually, Senator Johnson came in super early this morning and said he had a hunch you might be stopping by! He's waiting for you, ma'am. Go right down the hall and through the main doors into his office."

. . .

"Double it." McDermott said bluntly, after sitting silently across the coffee table from Senator Johnson for several awkward moments.

"Double what, Lois?"

"The number of refugees. Five thousand a year is nothing. Make it ten a year for five years. Fifty thousand orphans to be placed with American families."

Johnson folded his hands in his lap and looked around the room. "It's too early for Johnnie Walker Black, isn't it?"

McDermott didn't respond. She was all business. She knew that she would have only one shot to negotiate this deal and leverage her position.

"Fifty thousand, Lois? Is that what you want? Done. Fifty

thousand. Do we have a deal?"

"Almost."

Johnson stood up and paced around to the other side of his desk impatiently. "What else?"

"Not some special visa. Not residency. Citizenship. For all of them. As soon as they touch down on American soil."

"Lots of people are patiently waiting their turn in line for citizenship. Everyone has a soft spot in their heart for orphans, but magically making them all citizens would cause more problems than you think. Permanent residency is the right play here. Trust me."

McDermott stood. "Okay. Well, thanks for your time then."

Johnson moved closer to his colleague and smiled. "Why is this point so important?"

"Because anything less than citizenship would be insulting. We're going to milk the hell out of this for every drop of PR we can get from it. 'Hey, look at us. Look at all the kids we're saving.' Actually making them citizens seems only appropriate. Wouldn't you agree?"

"Perhaps. At least it does when you put it like that."

"Then you agree that any refugee agreement concerning orphans would need to include citizenship, right?"

"Yes, Lois. But we still need to ensure proper vetting—"

McDermott cut him off. "Give me a break. Every one of them will be six or under. Innocent kids. The easiest people in the world to vet."

"Not exactly, Lois. But I'm not here to quibble over the vetting of children. I can make this happen and still satisfy the hawks. Leave that part to me."

"Citizenship is a big one. Don't you have to talk to people about that one before you can okay it?"

"The president has given me wide discretion to accomplish some very specific goals. Consider it done. Now do we have a deal?"

McDermott walked past Johnson's desk and browsed the books on the shelves against the back wall of his office. "Almost."

"For God's sake, Lois. What is it?"

"We announce the refugee program first. At least a few days before the vote."

"No way. We vote to confirm Midas first. Then we announce the new program a week or so later. We've been working to fill that SCOTUS seat for over two hundred days. A lot of other things hinge on it. I cannot budge on that particular, Lois. Midas gets confirmed first. Then we can roll out your program with as much fanfare as you want. You're just going to have to trust me."

"In that case, I need a personal favor for a refugee I met at the camp. Her name is Asha. Her husband drowned when they tried to cross the Mediterranean. She's pregnant and has nothing. I made a promise that I'd help her. I'll go along with the vote for Midas first and trust you on the refugee program later, but I need Asha to be granted asylum immediately. Can you do that for me?"

"Just the woman? No one else?"

"Just Asha and her unborn child. Asylum, not citizenship."

"Done. I'll have them in the states with a week."

"And there's a human trafficker I want stopped. His name is Ahab."

"Ahab?"

"Yes. I've been trying to get an international arrest warrant but keep coming up against roadblocks. I want him out of business forever. Can you promise me that?"

"Why this one guy?"

"Because I made a promise that I intend to keep. Now you promise me—give me your word that you have the authority to green-light this program with full citizenship for the orphans. And that it will happen soon—not at some distant future date. I want your solemn word as Majority Leader, Senator Johnson. No games."

"You have better," he answered, pulling a small cellphone from his front pocket. He pressed several keys and held the phone to his ear. "You have my word as a Southern gentleman, which should be more than enough. But just in case there is any remaining doubt, let's get you a second opinion."

McDermott tried to maintain her poker face, but she was curious as to whom he could call so early in the morning to demonstrate that he had the authority to deliver on what he was promising.

"Yes, sir. ... Good morning, sir. ... She's right here in my office. ... Yes, sir, I think she'd like that very much." Johnson slowly extended his arm and offered McDermott the phone. "President Calhoun."

McDermott took the phone and paced to the window behind Johnson's desk. On the outside she may have looked calm, but inside she felt as if she was exploding. She took several deep breaths to calm her nerves.

Breathe. Keep it together. Just another day at the office, Lois. Just another day.

Then she turned her back on the Majority Leader, raised the phone to her ear, and greeted the President of the United States. "Good morning, Mr. President."

"Good morning to you too, Senator McDermott. The American people sure are lucky to have leaders like you and Senator Johnson—up at the crack of dawn, working together to solve problems. It's so refreshing to see that true bipartisanship is not dead and I hope we start to see much more of it in Washington, don't you?"

"That would be refreshing indeed, Mr. President."

"Listen, you'll have to forgive my boorishness, but I have another urgent matter I must attend to so I can't chat right now. But once things settle down at the end of the legislative session, we'd love to have you and your ... partner ... or whomever you'd like to bring with you over to the White House for dinner."

McDermott rolled her eyes at the president's awkward word choice.

"Thank you for the offer, sir. But for now—"

"For now you need assurances. Yes, I know. So let me be very clear. Senator Johnson has my full backing. Any promises he makes are backed up by me and the full power of my office. You have my word on that. He speaks very highly of you, by the way. He always has."

McDermott turned around and faced Johnson while she listened to President Calhoun.

"They're gonna make things tough on you for this, Senator. Just remember that it'll pass. Things always do."

The line went dead. McDermott handed the phone back to Johnson and took several deep breaths. She was starting to get dizzy but didn't want to sit down out of fear that she wouldn't be able to get back up.

The president is right. People are going to make things very rough for me for doing this. It's going to get bad. But fifty thousand suffering children will get loving parents. And I might get to spend time during my final years with Megan and Mark and Luci and the twins—like a real family.

McDermott's final decision was not an easy one. It was more a matter of choosing your pain. Prepare for the overwhelming backlash that will surely come after she votes to confirm Judge Midas, or prepare for a lifetime of knowing she could have delivered fifty thousand kids to deserving families and brought her own family closer together.

Make a decision and accept the consequences, Lois.

She extended her hand to Johnson to seal the deal.

"Done. Let's do this."

CHAPTER ELEVEN: Change of Mission

"A group of eager citizens reportedly called out to Benjamin Franklin as he was leaving the Constitutional Convention. 'Dr. Franklin, what kind of government have we been given by the delegates?' Franklin replied, 'A republic, if you can keep it.' "

Mark was listening to Senator Johnson's spiel through his earbuds. He pushed his keyboard, mouse, and paperwork to the side so he could clean the Heckler and Koch VP9 sitting on his desk. When he finished, he retrieved the M4 carbine from a standup safe and started breaking it down.

"Do you know what he meant with that answer, Mr. Landry?"

"What answer, sir?"

"Franklin's answer. A republic, *if* you can keep it," he said, emphasizing the *if*.

"No."

"Franklin knew that every republic throughout history had eventually failed, and he couldn't have been naïve enough to think the U.S. would be any different. But he knew we could stave off that day as long as enough good men were willing to make tough decisions and occasionally do unpleasant things when the circumstances called for them. Men like us, Mr. Landry. That means we have a tremendous responsibility. Would you agree?"

"Of course."

"Good. The PMC Wall should no longer be an issue for you. A courier will deliver your credentials to your home later today. I'll be moving offices within just a few weeks. Things will happen quickly after that. You'll be busy hunting down Oleg Borodin and destroying his network of spies, criminals, hackers, and God knows whoever else the Kremlin is using to sabotage the West. You have a lot of autonomy now—not quite like the autonomy Rome extended to Pompey the Great, but the closest thing we've got these days. Which means there usually won't be anyone looking over your shoulder. My advice is to take that power seriously and never do anything unless you're sure you'll be able to live with it."

Got it. Dunbar used to say the same thing. This stuff isn't new to me.

"Understood, Senator."

"You're also responsible for the decisions your people make in the field."

Okay. That part is new. Noted.

Johnson explained that Mark's team would continue to use the Imperium brand as cover. Mark already knew how he wanted to restructure the organization to meet the demands of its newest and only client: the National Security Advisor and—through him—the President of the United States. It would require moving some people around, but he was confident he could have everything up and running within a few short weeks. Maybe sooner. He had also already lined up meetings with the FBI, CIA, DEA, and NSA to get briefed on Borodin and his networks as much as possible.

"Welcome aboard, Mark. I have the highest expectations for you and I know you won't let me or the president down. I'm also very happy that you've shown your readiness to work on pressing domestic political affairs when necessary. And I'm impressed with what you've delivered. Don't be surprised if we need to go back to that well sometime in the future. That's all for now. I'll speak with you soon, Mr. Landry."

The line went dead. Mark removed his earbuds. Then he reassembled his rifle and performed a quick function check. All good. He turned his attention to the first planned op of the newly reconstituted Family, operating as Imperium.

Mark and a hand-picked team of Imperium operators had an overseas seek-and-destroy mission to conduct. And since Johnson had torn down the PMC Wall, they had all the resources they needed at their fingertips. That was an obvious reason for Mark to get out of the office and into the field again. Mark was a player-manager, as Dunbar had always been.

Dunbar.

Mark looked at the bare walls of his office and wondered when Dunbar had slipped in and out of the Imperium offices. All his things were gone. He had left nothing behind except a miniature model of a single-engine Piper Cub, similar to the one he had unexpectedly learned to fly solo on as a young operator in Vietnam almost half a century ago.

Classic Dunbar. I hope you're face down on a massage table somewhere, but I know better. God only knows what could be on that man's bucket list.

Mark returned his rifle to the safe as someone knocked and then opened his office door. It was Kenny.

"You got a minute?" he asked.

"Sure. Just trying to finish up a few things before I head home to spend time with Luci and the twins before heading out on this op. What's up? You're not about to tell me something crazy about your past, are you?"

Kenny smirked. "No. And I already promised, there's nothing else that would surprise you. But whenever you want to start sharing your past, I'm all ears."

"My past isn't nearly as exciting as yours, Kenny."

"Really? Then tell me about Berlin. I'm up for a boring story."

Mark parried the jab and changed the subject.

"What's next for you and Patty? Anything planned?"

"Actually, we're talking about eventually taking some time off to visit Atlanta together."

Kenny sat down in one of the chairs facing the big monitor on Mark's wall.

"Meeting the parents? Big step."

"No, it's not me meeting the parents." Kenny seemed embarrassed.

"It's not. Do they live in Atlanta too?"

"Yes."

"Staying at their place, I imagine?"

"Probably."

"How is that not meeting the parents?"

"I don't know. This kind of stuff is new to me, Mark. But it's also a little scary."

"What are you afraid of? That you might end up with a great family?"

Kenny stood up and paced around to stand next to Mark on the other side of his desk. "No. Ending up with a great family doesn't scare me. Losing them does. I've had family before and I lost them. And I don't ever want to relive that pain. Maybe that's why I'm being such a pussy."

"A pussy? Kenny, you are many things—impatient, sarcastic, and occasionally reckless, to name a few—but you are most definitely not a pussy. You've been through some tough times. It's normal to not want to repeat them."

"I guess that's why I look at you and scratch my head sometimes."

"Me? How come?" Mark asked as he started packing his things to go home.

"I lost both my parents and would do anything to have them back—to have grandparents for my future kids—but I can't. You have McDermott. She's your mother. Yet you keep her at a distance from you and your family. It's none of my business, but I've never understood why. She seems like a perfectly decent person."

Mark grabbed the last of his things and slung his bag over his shoulder. "She is. By all accounts she is a decent person, Kenny. But from the beginning of our relationship, I always felt like she was holding something back from me. Lying, perhaps. It was always just a hunch.

166

But that hunch was recently confirmed when she visited the refugee camp."

Kenny looked confused.

"I don't get it. What had she been lying about?"

Mark placed his bag on the floor at his feet and walked back behind his desk. He started tapping the keyboard and dragging things around on the wall monitor with the mouse. "I'll tell you what, Kenny. Let's see if you can figure it out. Since I've learned so much I never knew about you lately, it's only fair you get the chance to learn something new about me." Mark pointed to the wall monitor. "I've collected the dots for you. Now see if you can connect them. These are the only three files you need. Figure out what she lied to me about and I'll find a spot for you on this first op."

Kenny sprung out of his seat and approached the monitor to look at the three files.

The first contained Senator McDermott's comprehensive security plans from her covert visit to the refugee camp.

The second file was Mark Landry's own emergency medical information.

The third was information on Mark's biological father, Theodore "Teddy" Cartwright. It included the official reports from the helicopter crash that took his life as well as Cartwright's military records from the few months he had spent on active duty.

Kenny spent several minutes scrolling through the first few pages of each file. When he turned around, Mark had already left. He returned to the files and dug deeper, reading and rereading for half an hour before taking a break.

In the kitchen, he found leftover chicken wings and boneless spareribs from the China Wok. He thought about the files while the wings and ribs slowly heated up in the microwave.

Might as well have a snack while I wait for that.

Kenny grabbed a stale Dunkin' Donuts bagel from the counter and held it in the palm of one hand while he sawed it in half with the other.

What does he have against McDermott? What did she deceive him about?

"Shit!" He cut through the bagel and nicked the palm of his hand just enough to draw blood. "Dammit."

He stopped the microwave and headed toward the restroom to wash his hands and look for a band aid.

Mark's info. McDermott's info. Teddy's info. Everything I need is there, he says. So what's there? What do I have? Two parents and one child. Three blood relatives.

Kenny stopped dead in his tracks.

Blood.

Then he spun around and quickly headed back to Mark's office. This time he opened each file and went directly to each of their blood types, beginning with Mark's father.

According to Teddy Cartwright's initial U.S. Army physical and official autopsy, his blood type was O. Then he scrolled through McDermott's emergency medical information data sheet. Her blood type was also listed as O.

Finally, he scrolled through Mark's emergency medical information. Kenny knew what was coming. Mark's blood type was listed as A.

Holy shit. Two parents with Type O blood cannot make a baby with Type A blood. This guy Cartwright can't possibly be Mark's father. Why did she lie? Did she think he would never figure it out?

Kenny pulled out his phone to send a text message to Mark.

. . .

Mark laid down on the couch with Luci and looked down at the twins laying on the floor with the dog. The kids were watching a Disney movie. Murphy was watching the large bowl of popcorn on the floor between them.

"Daddy, why does Murphy keep farting?" asked Amanda.

"Because he's a dog, Mandy. That's what they do."

Luci elbowed Mark in the ribs. "Who wants ice cream?" she asked.

"Me!" replied the twins excitedly, each raising a hand above their heads.

Luci rolled over onto her side and wrapped her arms around her husband. "I'll take mine with jimmies. Should we pause the movie for you?"

"Uh, no. That won't be necessary. I'm pretty sure the fish ends up finding his dad or gets eaten by a shark. I'm good either way."

Mark's phone vibrated in his front pocket as he got up from the sofa. It was a text from Kenny.

KENNY: Holy shit. Lied about father? She must have one hell of a good reason.

MARK: Can't worry about that now. Too many other more urgent matters like our first op. You in?

Mark imagined Kenny beaming with pride at earning his spot on a special mission like this one. He was starting to send more information when an encrypted phone call came through from an unknown overseas number. He answered on his way to the kitchen.

"Mark Landry."

After a few seconds of silence, he heard Heike's voice. "*Guten abend*, Mark."

He walked straight through the kitchen, opened the sliding glass door, and stepped out onto the back deck. "Hello, Heike."

"I am sorry to bother you, Mark. I imagine you are at home spending time with your beautiful family. But I figured you would want to know that a short time ago Oleg Borodin boarded a plane in Prague and he is heading here."

"Where's here?"

"Berlin, Mark. His plane lands in less than an hour. I know you are interested in this man for things he has done in your country. Would you like us to detain him when he arrives?"

Mark thought for a minute before answering. If Borodin was traveling outside of Russia already, he must be reasonably sure that nobody had connected him to the incident in Boston. He didn't need the Germans to detain him now. It would be better if they simply surveilled him and made the information available to Mark and his team.

"No, let him through. But can you keep an eye on him for me while he's there?

"Of course, Mark. A professional courtesy of this magnitude would usually require a more formal request. But in light of your recent career promotion, consider it a congratulatory present."

How does she know about that?

"What else can you share with me about Borodin?"

"He lives in Anapa, south Russia near the Black Sea. From there he manages global networks of spies, informants, hackers, and thugs for the FSB. In spite of the incident in Boston, we never expected him to stay in America very long. He never stays anywhere very long. In fact, he has been assigned to three different embassies this year alone. He shows up, organizes things quickly, then moves on. Our intelligence regarding Russian mafia and FSB networks throughout Europe is much more comprehensive, but I'm afraid it would require a meeting."

"Okay, when are you in town again?"

"No, Mark. It would require a meeting here—in Berlin."

Mark looked up at the sky and shook his head in disbelief.

I knew it. I knew when she walked out of the bar that it wouldn't be the last time I saw her. I just didn't think it would be this soon.

"My schedule is pretty tight but I can try to put together a trip—"

"You can do whatever you wish, Mark. Just know that the French are also looking for this man. If they show up first, I can't make any guarantees—"

Mark cut her off. "Don't do that, Heike. I'll be there soon, okay? There are a few pressing matters I need to attend to personally. After that, I'll make plans to go to Berlin."

"You mean return to Berlin, don't you, Mark? A sort of homecoming, *ja?*"

"Something like that. I'll be in touch."

"And I will be here waiting for you, Mark."

I know you will.

Mark ended the call and put his phone back into his front pocket. Then he went back into the house and called out for his dog. "Murphy, come here, boy!" Murphy came running around the corner from the family room at top speed and slid to a stop in front of his master. "You wanna go for a ride? Yeah? You wanna go on a trip?"

CHAPTER TWELVE: Pompeius Magnus

Ahab had left half of his crew behind with the ship and brought the other half with him to the edge of the designated refugee areas. There, they collected payments ahead of the next morning's illegal boat trip into the Mediterranean. The boat could hold 150 people safely. Ahab collected money from over 300.

"Get in the truck. We're going back to the boat," he barked. Then he waddled around to the passenger door and climbed up into the cab of the truck, using mostly his arm strength.

On the way back, he slapped and cursed his driver for slowing down and turning to avoid a stray dog in the middle of the road. "I said don't stop for anything, you idiot! Not while I have all this money. Especially not for a fucking dog," he scowled.

Ahab was not worried about any legal authority figures. They could be paid off. But he was concerned with the ever-present threat posed by other opportunistic criminals in the area. As a security measure, he rotated his operation through several compounds along the coast. The compound he chose for tonight was his favorite. It consisted of a docking area for the 100-foot boat, a bunkhouse for his 10-member crew, and a private cabin for himself—all cut off from the world by a 10-foot high stone wall. Ahab told the men to get out of the truck and laid down the rules for the night.

He told the crew members not to leave the compound. He knew that if he didn't keep the men on a short leash, there was a good chance that at least half of them would get into some kind of trouble. They'd either get too drunk to crew the boat, fight with rival thugs, or both. They could still drink and play cards all night, but no leaving the compound. At sunup, hundreds of refugees would be crawling over each other to get a spot on the boat and the crew needed to be ready for them.

Ahab stood on the wooden steps of his cabin, tilted his head back, and filled his nostrils with the smell coming from the bunkhouse. Someone was cooking dinner. He yelled to one of his men to fetch him some of whatever it was. Then he pulled his satellite phone from his back pocket. He pressed the power button and lifted the receiver to his ear.

He might as well have put a gun to his head and pulled the trigger.

The MC-12W Liberty Intelligence, Surveillance, and Reconnaissance (ISR) aircraft circling above at fifteen thousand feet picked up the signal from the satellite phone and pinpointed Ahab's location. Voice recognition confirmed his identity. From that moment he was tagged. He could run, but he could not hide anymore.

The Liberty aircraft operators reported their find. Less than an hour later, two unmarked MH-60 Black Hawks lifted off from a U.S. naval vessel patrolling the Mediterranean and headed toward land. Mark rode in the lead aircraft. Kenny sat behind and across from him to coordinate the cyber elements of the raid. Billy, Sadie, and the new guy, David, each led a team of three operators.

Ten of the most skilled operators in the world, plus Kenny, against Ahab and his misfit crew of ten.

When they were fifteen minutes from land, Mark keyed his communications headset and spoke into the whisper mic hovering just a few millimeters from his lips. "Clear the air."

The surrounding airspace would be closed to all other traffic by the time they arrived at Ahab's compound. Nobody would see the helicopters coming with naked eyes or radar—they were flying in blackout mode and employing advanced stealth technology to mask their movement. Nor would anybody be alarmed by the noise—United Nations and NGO aircraft were often active in the area. Besides, these were not normal Black Hawks being flown by normal pilots. They were highly classified, modified versions of the Black Hawk outfitted with the latest aeronautic noise reduction technology; and they were being flown by pilots from Task Force Brown (also known as the Night Stalkers from the 160th Special Operations Aviation Regiment out of Fort Campbell, Kentucky).

Unfortunately, there wasn't enough flat area for both Black Hawks to land together. Mark's helicopter would be able to land about fifty yards from Ahab's cabin, so his group would exit the aircraft on their own, but the group of operators in the other aircraft would have to fast-rope to the ground between the bunkhouse and boat.

According to satellite feeds and real-time surveillance intelligence from the MC-12W Liberty, Ahab was in his cabin and the men were split evenly between the bunkhouse and boat. Earlier, there had been a one-man roving security detail on the deck of the boat. Now that man was seated with his head bowed and a rifle across his lap. Passed out. There were no other visible sentries, but each crew member was presumed to be armed. The eyes in the sky would keep the operators informed of all movement within the compound—all in real time.

Mark's orders were to take control of the compound through overwhelming force and violent action. Some of the crew and perhaps even Ahab would die during the initial assault, but the Imperium team would need to take a few of them alive. Someone would have to load their dead counterparts into the boat for the grand finale that Mark had planned for Ahab's vile human trafficking business. "A version of the Viking funeral," Mark called it.

Mark looked back at Kenny, who was tapping away at his mobile workstation mounted firmly on the frame of the Black Hawk. *Is he smiling?*

"Kenny, you wanna tell me what the fuck is so funny?"

Kenny heard Mark's voice in his headset and looked up at his boss, smiling and shaking his head. "Yeah, I was just thinking. Back when I was the Hobbit, I spent a lot of time looking over my shoulder for the guys in the black helicopters who might wanna come snatch me up. Now I'm one of the guys in the black helicopter. It's kinda fucked up when you think about it."

Mark looked out over the nose of the helicopter. Then he spoke into the mic again so that Kenny could hear him.

"There's a first time for everything. I have a funny feeling the ex-Hobbit might even see his first dragon tonight."

"What do you mean?"

Mark pulled panoramic night vision goggles onto his head and tightened the straps.

"Nothing. We're five minutes out, Kenny. Start your magic."

. . .

Ahab was almost asleep when the small electric motor that powered his ceiling fan stopped humming. The fan spun slower and slower before finally stopping. He lay there on the dingy cot, hoping it was just one of the regular blackouts that last only a few moments. Beads of perspiration began to form on his forehead and upper lip. He cleaned the sweat with his hands, then wiped them on his soiled mattress.

He checked the time and reached for the phone on the wooden crate that he used as a nightstand. He was going to call one of the guys in the bunkhouse to see if they had lost electricity too. He rubbed his eyes and focused on the small screen.

Dead. No service bars—cell or data.

He slowly got to his feet. Then he limped across the room and flipped the light switch. Nothing. Ahab steadied himself against the wall and peered out the window in the direction of the bunkhouse and boat. No lights. He wondered why nobody had started the backup generator. Where was the guard?

He knew something was not right.

. . .

When they were two minutes out, Mark addressed the young operator strapped in next to Kenny. He pointed to Murphy. The dog's tactical harness was attached to the operator's vest with a carabiner. "Be sure to take care of him. And remember, he's used to being right next to me, so you need to make it clear that you're the boss tonight."

The experienced former U.S. Marine Corps dog handler gave a thumbs-up and stroked Murphy with a gloved hand. The German shepherd was panting anxiously. Before the skids touched down, the operators all took one last look at their individual tactical displays for real-time images of their targets.

Mark's group hit the ground running. He, the dog handler, and another operator went for Ahab's cabin. Meanwhile, the other two maneuvered to provide cover for Billy's group as they fast-roped to the ground and kept an eye on the main entrances to the bunkhouse and the boat. When the last set of boots touched soil, the second Black Hawk sprang into the air, banked hard left, and circled back around to an overwatch position above the compound—well outside the line of fire should the AC-130U Spooky II gunship circling above need to engage targets.

Max could hear Sadie's team assaulting the bunkhouse as he and two other operators were quickly ascending the boat's wooden boarding ramp. The passed-out sentry awoke and clumsily leaned over the side of the boat to check on the commotion. Billy reflexively raised his suppressed Sig Sauer M400 and sent two rounds into the man's face and throat. His limp body tumbled over the edge and splashed into the water. Billy motioned one of his operators toward the only hatch, which led to a small room with bunk beds inside the belly of the ship where the remaining crew members were sleeping.

"Ready when you are," Billy said into his headset.

The operator removed a flashbang grenade from his tactical belt. He pulled the pin and lobbed it through the open hatch. The MK 9-banger bounced on the steep metal stairs before landing in the middle of the room with a thud. The operators turned away from the door to shield themselves from the nine consecutive blinding flashes and intensely loud bangs that were about to go off inside the metal container. Then they simply waited with their weapons trained on the hatch.

Sadie's voice came over the team's headsets. "Bunkhouse secure."

Billy's team let the first two shellshocked men stumble through the hatch and onto the deck of the boat. Both were blinded. The man closest to the 9-banger had two ruptured eardrums. Billy butt-stroked both men with his rifle, dragged them kicking and screaming to the side, and motioned for one of his operators to zip-tie their hands and check for weapons. He then told the operator to wait in place. He would much rather wait for the final two enemy combatants to climb out on their own and deal with them on deck than have to go in and get them.

Less than a minute later, the first disoriented man passed through the hatch waving a 12-gauge pump-action shotgun around in front of him like a rookie fireman trying to keep control of his hose. One of Mark's operators fired three rounds in rapid succession into the man's chest. He dropped the shotgun and continued for several more steps before collapsing. Then he began crawling, scratching, and clawing his way like a mortally wounded animal, trying to get to the edge of the boat, all while screaming at the top of his lungs. The operator silenced him with one more round through the head and waited for the final man to emerge.

Just as Mark's team reached the door to Ahab's cabin, the voice of one of the MC-12W Liberty's crew members came through his headset.

"We just lost visual on Ahab. There's a table in the northeast corner of the cabin. He just disappeared under it. Probably went underground."

"Roger," Mark replied. "Possibly an escape tunnel. I'm sending in the dog. Just in case, keep an eye out for him to emerge somewhere nearby." Then he turned to the dog handler. "Send him in."

Mark twisted the knob and pushed the cabin door open. The handler reached down and released the leash from Murphy's harness. Then he gave a loud command, telling the dog to enter the room and bite anything that moved. Murphy's adrenaline surged at the prospect of finding a bad guy to bite. He flew through the open door of the single-room cabin in a barking frenzy.

Mark and the handler looked at their tactical displays to watch the live feed from the camera mounted on Murphy's harness. The room appeared empty, but they gave the dog a few minutes to sniff around for explosives before entering. When they did, Murphy was sniffing a piece of plywood on the floor under the table. He stopped barking and pointed his tail straight back. He had found something.

Under the plywood was a five-foot-deep entrance to a tunnel about the width of a whiskey barrel. One of the operators fed a piece of cable with a microscopic camera on the end into the dark hole and spun it around to get a bird's-eye view. It appeared to go straight for about twenty feet before turning hard right.

Mark looked at Murphy. "What do you think, Murph? You wanna go in there and bite this asshole?" He nodded to the handler and moved back to the cabin door so he could look out over the rest of the compound. Sadie had already reported that the bunkhouse was secure. Two survivors. Mark asked Billy if the boat was secure yet. He heard two shots coming from the direction of the water, followed by Billy's voice in his headset.

"It is now."

Mark filled everyone in on the tunnel situation and told them to start consolidating the crew onto Ahab's boat. Then he turned his attention to Murphy's tactical camera. The dog was methodically working his way through the tunnel, sniffing for explosives and someone to bite. After making the hard right turn, he picked up a scent and quickened his pace. Murphy could hear his handler encouraging him through the small speaker attached to his harness.

Then he started barking ferociously and quickened his pace to a controlled run. After turning another corner, he took off sprinting. Mark squinted at his screen to try to determine what the dog saw. Then Murphy suddenly stopped and leaped straight up into the air toward the man, who was squeezing his way through a narrow escape hatch above.

Murphy sank his teeth into Ahab's right thigh and clamped down as hard as he could with his powerful jaws and no plans to let go. He dangled in the air, shaking his head back and forth furiously.

Mark and the handler waited for the screams, but they never came.

Murphy continued to clamp down and tear away at Ahab. But the vile trafficker of human beings didn't make a sound. When Ahab reached down toward the cargo pockets of his pants, Mark thought he may be reaching for a weapon to use on the dog. He wasn't.

Murphy fell to the ground and landed on his back with a leg in his mouth—Ahab's prosthetic leg. Then he looked up and barked as the one-legged fugitive shimmied his way out the escape hatch. Mark and the handler looked at each other.

"You gotta be shitting me," Mark said.

The handler recalled Murphy. As the dog made his way back through the tunnel to the main cabin, the eye in the sky reported new movement.

"Be advised, it looks like we have one individual emerging from a tunnel approximately one hundred yards northeast of your location. Just one so far. Stand by."

Mark retrieved the dog from the tunnel and exited the cabin to look northeast. He could see Ahab, less than a football field away, crawling out of the tunnel on his belly. Ahab steadied himself against a large rock to stand on his one good leg and started hopping toward the main gate of the compound. He fell flat on his face, got up, and started hopping again.

Mark pulled the red, high-powered, handheld tactical laser from its pouch on the front of his duty belt. He projected the red dot onto Ahab with one hand. Then he pulled Murphy in tight with the other hand and drew his attention downrange. He made small circles on Ahab's back with the red laser.

"You see it, Murph? You see it? Yeah? Got it? Go get 'em!"

Murphy took off barking and sprinting at top speed across the rocky dirt terrain that lay between him and his target. He arrived just as

Ahab was struggling to get onto his feet once again. The dog attacked just as he had been trained—not by flying through the air uncontrollably, but by slowing his approach at the last instant and then arching up to bite the target's thigh or upper arm. Murphy opted for the top of Ahab's arm near the shoulder.

Ahab's desperate shrieks pierced the nighttime air as Murphy's teeth clamped onto his flesh. Mark held up a hand to the handler. "Give him a minute. He's earned it and this asshole's gonna die tonight anyway."

. . .

"That's a lot of money," said Billy. "Is that everything?"

Mark looked at the ammo crates filled with cash, jewelry, and anything else of value that Ahab could exploit from the refugees looking to cross the Mediterranean. "I think there's more in the tunnel. It's impossible to get this money back to all the right people, but the agency supposedly has someone here they trust enough to redistribute it adequately."

Billy rolled his eyes.

"Yeah, no shit. But that's not our problem and I want to get the fuck out of here. We'll leave the chosen one with the cash. Once the agency picks it up, he's free to go. Let's just make sure he can see the fireworks from here and knows his job."

"Roger. He's on the dock."

Mark and Billy started walking toward the boat. The rest of the Imperium team had already set fire to the bunkhouse and cabin. The surviving crew members were carrying their dead shipmates into the belly of the boat. When the last man had descended the metal staircase, Mark motioned for David to close and lock the hatch.

Mark looked at the team member who was serving as translator, then at the crew member Billy had chosen to spare—a skinny man in his mid-thirties. He was seated on the dock with his arms tied behind his back. Murphy was seated next to him. Murphy's teeth were only inches away from the man, and his chest was damp from his own saliva.

Mark knelt down and slowly tapped the tip of his index finger on the man's forehead as he spoke.

"You deserve to die today. You know that, right?"

The young criminal nodded his head. He tried to appear as if he had it together, but on the inside he was terrified. The jacked-up, eighty-pound German shepherd just inches from his face did not help.

"I know exactly who you are and can find you any time I want," Mark lied. "You understand that, right?"

The man nodded more furiously, evoking a deep growl from Murphy.

Mark reflected on something Dunbar had taught him years earlier. "The Vikings never actually drank from the skulls of their enemies. But they sure loved the fact that their enemies were convinced they did." Then he gave his instructions to the translator.

This crew member would be the only one to survive. In exchange, he would be expected to spread the word far and wide to every trafficker in the area that they risked meeting the same fate if they did not cease operations immediately. Mark knew that it was no permanent solution and that many of them would simply stay quiet for a while before reopening their doors. But many others would consider the risk—and the horror experienced by Ahab's outfit—and take heed. The more graphic the survivor's accounting, the better.

Mark checked his watch as he walked up the ramp and looked over the boat's railing. Ahab was sprawled on the deck, pushing furiously with his one good leg to get away, but moving only in circles due to the chain padlocked tightly around his neck on one end, the other end secured to the deck. Mark nodded his head with approval. Then Kenny's voice came over his headset. "Mark, they're not going to keep this airspace restricted forever."

"Adios, Ahab." Mark turned and headed toward his waiting Black Hawk for extraction. He spoke to Sadie on the way. "Leave two men with the boat. Have them drive it out a few thousand meters. You can pull 'em up from there."

. . .

Kenny watched the burning compound get smaller and smaller out the side window of Mark's Black Hawk. Then he looked and gave a thumbs-up to Mark. "Fewer scumbags in the world, right?"

"Almost."

When the last of Sadie's operators had been extracted from the boat by fast-rope and both were safely hooked into their seats inside the Black Hawk, she gave a thumbs-up to the pilot and pressed the talk button on her headset. "The boys are back in the nest, Mark."

Mark changed frequencies and initiated contact with the AC-130U Spooky II's fire control officer, who was monitoring the operation closely from several thousand feet overhead. He relayed the location of the boat and waited for confirmation.

"Roger, we have a visual on the vessel."

"Stand by to engage," instructed Mark. Then he tapped Kenny on the knee. "Look out the other window. Remember the dragon I mentioned earlier? It's about to breathe fire."

Kenny read Mark's lips as he spoke into his headset. "Cleared to engage."

The AC-130U Spooky II fired from above with the 20mm and 40mm guns. A thick stream of orange tracer fire poured down like hot lava onto Ahab's boat. Bullets ripped through the vessel. Several fuel tanks exploded sending pieces of the boat flying through the air. Then dark smoke billowed from the target as it filled with water and sunk into the dark Mediterranean waters.

Kenny was gazing out the window in awe. Mark adjusted his settings so they could speak privately.

"What do you think?" he asked.

Kenny shook his head back and forth. He was mesmerized.

"It's beautiful."

The Next Mark Landry Novel

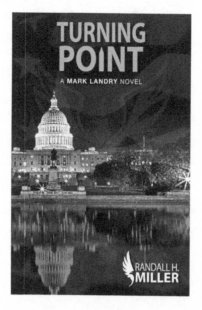

The Amazon best-selling Mark Landry series continues with Turning Point--a contemporary thriller driven by a high-tech special operations manhunt, family upheaval, and multiple crises confronting intelligence personnel on two continents.

When the President and National Security Advisor want Oleg Borodin--legendary Russian spy and master of disinformation-- eliminated, Mark Landry gets the call. Mark and his team of operators scour the globe in a gripping pursuit that quickly turns deadly. Back home in Massachusetts, Mark's wife, Detective Sergeant Luci Landry, is on the verge of retirement and contemplating a run for sheriff until unexpected events threaten her reputation and her future.

Turning Point intertwines real-life issues with shocking plot twists to keep you on the edge of your seat, wondering what will happen next--and questioning everything you thought you knew. Turning Point picks up the story from Wrong Town and Family Matters.

About the Author

Thanks again for reading my book! I hope you enjoyed it. If you did, please recommend it to others by word of mouth and social media, and consider leaving a review online. Positive reviews from readers like you have a tremendous impact on author rankings and search results. I personally appreciate your support. More important, you'll be doing your part to keep the Mark Landry books coming!

Thanks very much and stay safe! – Randall H. Miller

Twitter @randallHmiller

Visit Randall H. Miller's Facebook Page

Randall H. Miller is the author of seven books, including the Amazon Top 10 bestselling Mark Landry series. He has a M.A. in Diplomacy (focused on international terrorism) and a B.A. in Criminal Justice, both from Norwich University, the nation's oldest private military college. A former officer in the 82nd Airborne and 2nd Infantry Divisions, he researches and trains regularly in weapons and close-quarters battle tactics alongside law enforcement and military operators. He lives in North Andover, Massachusetts. www.RandallHMiller.com

Made in the USA
Coppell, TX
21 March 2021

52084504R10111